THE JUDGE'S HOUSE

THE JUDGE'S HOUSE

A Novel by
JONATHAN STRONG

Quale Press

Front cover image: *View of Bookshelves in Library (Room 202), Evergreen, 4545 North Charles Street, Baltimore, Independent City, MD*, photograph by James W. Rosenthal, courtesy of the Library of Congress

Back cover image: *Carved Steps, Front View (1939), Hampton Boon House, Fayette, Howard County, MO*, photograph by Piaget-van Ravenswaay, courtesy of the Library of Congress

Cover & interior design by Marinna Castilleja

ISBN: 978-1-935835-16-5
LCCN: 2015947827

www.quale.com

Contents

"The mint is there, and we know it;
yet our palate knows only the young potato."
—*George Gissing,* The Private Papers of Henry Ryecroft

THEIR NEIGHBOR

William Turley, the older gentleman who lived next door, slipped on a patch of black ice along his front walk and was carried in a passing pickup truck to the county hospital where Dr. Nancy Huggins now practiced. He died that afternoon, the 29th of December, 2008. The truck driver, quite shaken, brought the news back to Rockvale, to the courthouse, to the post office, to the police, even to the public library, and to the bank where Lawrence Huggins was the manager. When husband and wife, banker and pediatrician, met at home that evening, they had the same sad tale to tell.

Lawrence and Nancy were among the few black couples in the county and the sole professional one. They had moved out from Chicago two years ago when AmTrust absorbed the Sinnissippi County Bank and offered Lawrence, at last, a managership. Nancy had hated to abandon the urban population she felt responsible for, but there was a position at the county hospital she could fill for now. It was a foray into the rural white world such as their daughter Chloe was making for graduate school far up in Wisconsin. They hoped their stay would be equally brief and, after doing good service, they would be promoted back to Chicago to crown their working lives.

But the Hugginses had come to feel sufficiently at home in Rockvale to mingle unselfconsciously with storekeepers, patrons, and patients. Everyone was polite, to an extent even warm, but William Turley, the quiet old man next door, had taken them truly to heart. Late one afternoon some months after their arrival, they had encountered him on the sidewalk and, with a spontaneous neighborliness, proposed he join them for some simple home cooking. The postman had previously informed Lawrence that Mr. Turley never visited anyone's home, but astonishingly he accepted the invitation.

The old man, who declined mail delivery to his door, left his house only to empty his box at the post office or, Lawrence knew, to withdraw cash from the considerable bank account he kept, for some reason, at another AmTrust branch in the neighboring county. He also made use of the public library's computer, so the librarian had told Nancy, to order more for his collection of old books, and he might be seen carrying home a padded book mailer along with a small bag of groceries from the IGA or some bagged item from Freddy's Hardware. To any greeting Mr. Turley would respond with a plain how-de-do. He seemed to have no friend in all of Sinnissippi County.

Susie Gitchell, the librarian, had also told Nancy that William Turley had been reclusive ever since he came to town as a young man. Susie was then in sixth grade and often watched him from her bedroom window across the street while he tended his garden, now long lying fallow, or went out on his brief errands. Sometimes he would carry home a particularly heavy-looking carton of what the old postmistress told her were rare volumes the shy young man ordered from a well-known dealer in Chicago. As a girl, Susie had made up stories about William Turley. She asserted that he was rather attractive back then, with a pleasant softness not yet turned to bulk, but if they passed on the sidewalk all she had ever got from him was a nod or a slight smile. And that had still been true these many years later.

So before he arrived at the Hugginses' for that first supper, their neighbor was a considerable mystery to them. Why had he accepted their invitation? Perhaps he did not wish to appear racist by begging off. In everything that happened in this small new white world, Lawrence and Nancy naturally suspected an element of prejudice, even in the kindest gestures, perhaps especially in them. They kept at a certain remove, as did their other near neighbors. It was difficult to be entirely at ease with folks who had such little acquaintance with black people or cities. They anticipated a somewhat awkward evening with Mr. Turley, sequestered as he had long been in the dark brick Victorian house next door.

In outline, it was a near twin to their own, but of a rusty brown brick not creamy white clapboard. At night the Hugginses kept a light burning in every room while next door there was always but one lighted window on the second floor. The human silhouette on the drawn shade held an open book. At times it leaned forward or stretched back and gestured with one hand. Now and then it faded to a dimmer gray shadow standing or moving about, book still in hand. By daylight there was nothing to be seen over there at all, but on a hot summer afternoon behind a humming fan by an open window they could almost detect a reading voice, rising and falling with some degree of passion. And when the setting sun shone through the tall windows on the far side of the Turley house, the Hugginses caught an impression of a book-lined front parlor. But even after Will Turley had been their supper guest a dozen times, they knew no more of the interior of his house or what he did there all day or, for all their conversations, who the old man really was.

And now after nearly two years, on a late December evening, Nancy and Lawrence had to deliver to each other their reports of his death.

Nancy had heard a bustle out in the corridor when two orderlies, followed by the Good Samaritan truck driver, wheeled the dying man past on a gurney. Later, she asked at the front desk what had occurred. It seemed an elderly gentleman had cracked his head open on his icy front walk. He was in a coma but soon had been pronounced dead. The man who had driven him, the receptionist said, did odd jobs around town. "A sweet guy," she said, "named Henry Settle." When Dr. Nancy checked the hospital log she discovered the dead man's name and, sitting back in her consulting room, leaned her head on her arms and let the tears come.

From his office at the bank, Lawrence had heard a man's shaky voice talking to the tellers out front. He was saying how the dead man's wallet had in it only an AmTrust card and a card for the Rockvale library. The name was William Turley. "You know him, Millie," came the truck driver's voice. "He's the old gent from Phelps Street." "Oh, gosh, and you're the one that found him?" asked the teller. "Flat out on the cement walk," the shaky voice replied. Lawrence sat motionless at his desk, pressing his thumbs to his throbbing temples, and stayed like that for some minutes. He could not make himself get up to go ask for more details. He may not have known much about his neighbor of the last two years, but now he knew the one final thing: how the man's life had come to an end.

So Lawrence and Nancy Huggins, having finished their stories, embraced and then, without either suggesting it, put their winter coats back on, opened their front door, and went down the steps and across the frosted grass to locate that deceptive patch of ice. It was too dark to see more than a faint reflection from the streetlamp and nearby a darker splotch that might be frozen blood. They had never before ventured this far up William Turley's front walk. It was always out on the public sidewalk that they offered their invitations. Now, too late, they approached the house. Shadows of arborvitaes and yews fell across their path. They passed the front bay window and carefully stepped up to the side porch where a bare wistaria vine tangled around the railing and ran up the pillars. The brass "17" beside the door shone in the light from their own living room bay window. On the door was affixed a white-enamel oval bearing a picture of a nesting bird and the word "Whippoorwill," as if to name the house and not the man who had lived within it.

"Who can know what comes next in a life!" Lawrence said with his arm around his wife as they retreated.

"And this morning it was all melting," she said.

His Obituary

Next morning a light snow had covered the dangerous ice patch and any spots of blood that might show by day. On his walk to work, Lawrence stopped at the courthouse to inquire into the death of his neighbor. The hospital had notified the county clerk who had sufficient documentation—a deed and insurance records and tax forms—to enable him to contact the deceased's lawyer in the neighboring county, where they had transported the body. The next of kin—first cousins once removed who lived somewhere in the East—had been notified as well. "I know he maintained an AmTrust account, Mr. Huggins," the clerk said, "or I wouldn't be telling you this much, it being a private matter."

"I wonder," Lawrence ventured, "why he did his business at the Riparian branch. He only used ours to cash his checks, never even used the ATM."

"He was a strange old codger," said the clerk. "Hey, his lawyer mentioned something about having to contact you, Mr. Huggins. Between you and me," the clerk said leaning forward across the counter, "the fellow must've had a pile of dough. He never worked a day in his life. We should all be so lucky!"

Lawrence returned a commiserating smirk and made his way to the bank thinking how, back before the AmTrust takeover, that Riparian County bank bore no relation to the one here. Back then, local banks trusted folk enough to cash their out-of-town checks. For whatever reason, Will Turley had lived here in Sinnissippi County but kept his money in Riparian. He had not known that mergers and electronic banking would eventually moot his precautions.

Yesterday at her office, Nancy had chosen not to view the body, though she might have, but this morning she almost wished she had. Mr. Turley had been removed to a funeral home, and there was no service scheduled until the director heard from the distant relations. That was all they knew at the hospital. Throughout her day of caring for youngsters and their worried mothers, Nancy envisioned again and again old Will's head cracked open on the cold stone or, even before that, the fall itself, that last moment of his feet slipping out from under him and then the catapulting down as if the front walk was rising up to slam into his face as he teetered there for a final never-ending second. Nancy could not rid her mind of these visions, though she had seen the results of worse accidents many times in Chicago. And what if it had been on some other freezing night that Will, on his way over for supper, had slipped and fallen on their own front walk. They must always keep it sanded now and step more carefully themselves.

If there was to be no service, there would be no occasion to set aside these thoughts. Nancy had grown up in church as had Lawrence, so they had joined the Rockvale Methodist and on Sundays sat amongst its white parishioners. It was hardly a city church, but it had to do for now. Nancy hoped the pastor might say a few words on William Turley's passing, though Will had surely been no Methodist. Someone must say something. Could nothing be said?

Lawrence had the same concern. From his office he phoned up the editor of the weekly paper, who had learned of the death and already had prepared a brief notice. "Might I add something more personal?" Lawrence asked.

"We'd certainly welcome it, Mr. Huggins, but what could you possibly say? Did you know him at all?"

For half an hour Lawrence sat at his desk trying out sentences and then emailed the following words to the editor: "William Turley was a kindly friend to his neighbors and a deeply learned man who had read all the classics. He had a vast store of knowledge, and his quiet wisdom will be sorely missed."

The editor emailed back for permission to attribute the remarks to Mr. Lawrence Huggins, manager of AmTrust-Sinnissippi, but Lawrence replied that he did not wish to appear self-serving at such a time. Nonetheless, when the *Gazette* came out on Wednesday morning, there stood his name. He feared it would cause some people to resent the prominent position he held in their community. Many of them already seemed uneasy at the mention of the nation's first black president-elect. In 2006, when the Hugginses arrived in Rockvale, it was enough that Illinois had him as its U.S. senator.

THEIR NEW YEAR

On New Year's Eve, Nancy and Lawrence went out after work for a quiet dinner at the Basswood Restaurant but planned to stay home that evening when the town's teenagers would surely be cruising Courthouse Square, awaiting the midnight fireworks at the fairgrounds. The Hugginses had had their own true New Year's celebration watching Grant Park on election night and wishing they could have been in that mass of proud Chicagoans where they would have felt more at home than in their temporary living room in front of the TV.

Now they took their seats by the restaurant's riverside windows and ordered from a chubby waitress wearing a "2009" rhinestone tiara that embarrassed her, she said, but Mr. Bass had made her wear it tonight. While they sat looking out at the frozen river sipping their ice water, Lawrence could not help but wonder aloud if that man in the pickup truck, Henry Settle, would have stopped as readily if it had been one of them lying there bleeding on the cement. To be honest he probably would have, Lawrence admitted, but wasn't it natural to have some doubt? And if Settle had stopped for one of them, would he have been as kind? Well, perhaps doubly so, not to seem racist—an exceptionally Good Samaritan he would have been. "Better that sort than the other," Nancy said, "but I've not met this Henry, so I couldn't say."

Dinner at the Basswood was hearty in a small-town fancy way. After the doughy rolls and bowls of crisp salad came big slabs of red roast beef, red potatoes with mint sauce, overcooked French beans, and a slice of what their waitress called "Yorkster pudding." The Asti Spumante was festive enough, but this was certainly no Chicago.

Afterwards, they only had room for the lemon sherbet option and some decaf. It was quite chilly walking home. Nancy was thinking of the dark brick house next door and imagining the old man lying out there in his coma—for how long? Had the truck driver seen him fall and skidded to a stop or seen a strange big lump on the ground and slowed down for a closer look? Will Turley was a large man, hefty though not actually fat. He must have gone down with a whomp. And Lawrence was wondering if he had been on his way to pick up another carton of books at the post office or maybe to cash his final check of 2008.

Aside from noting the considerable balance, Lawrence had never investigated the Turley account, though he easily could have now that everything was AmTrust. Neither had Nancy inspected the old man's medical records. Their curiosity about their neighbor had never encouraged them to pry. But now they were each conceiving a deeper interest in him. He had relaxed with them in their house as had no other dinner guest from either bank or hospital or church. When Will Turley had found reason to mention their skin color, his tone betrayed no unease. He had talked of it and his own pale shade in a philosophical sense, never personal but rather as qualities to ponder about the odd human race. Their other guests would offer workplace chatter or droning tales of this son or that daughter or a new car or a dream vacation—politics never, religion only by implication, and money always in terms of an outrageous price or a fabulous deal. Will Turley stuck to larger themes, as if he had no personal life of his own and did not expect to hear mundane details from the Hugginses. "You must do a lot of reading," Nancy had once prodded. "Seems all I do is read," he answered, "but not to glean information. Merely to live in many other people's lives." "What's wrong with your own, Will?" Lawrence had dared to ask. "Other lives are my life" came his response.

Nancy and Lawrence had just stepped inside their front door when the phone rang. Chloe, up in Appleton, was wishing them a happy New Year early because she knew they would be sound asleep by ten. She was quite happy herself, with a promising new boyfriend known to her parents only as "Deet." They had learned he was twenty-seven and tall and smart as can be and much darker than Chloe. He taught theater, an unusual subject for a black man in northern Wisconsin, Lawrence thought.

Nancy was on duty early New Year's Day, and Lawrence always devoted January First to sorting out the previous year's expenditures and watching a little football. Sitting comfortably on the sofa with his laptop and paperwork arranged strategically on the coffee table and the huge flat-screen across the room shining cheerfully, his mind kept drawing him to the house next door, where he had never seen the glow of any sort of screen in any window. Every house in the town of Rockvale on a dim winter holiday would be flashing out blues and reds and yellows onto the falling snow, but Will Turley had no television and probably no radio or CD player either. Lawrence had heard no sounds from there but a whirring fan on hot days and the distant modulations of a deep voice reading aloud. And Will certainly had no computer, because he used the library's to search online for his old books. Lawrence had never even heard a phone ring or a doorbell, but who would have rung? A kid selling candy or magazine subscriptions might have climbed those steps—or a pair of Jehovah's Witnesses or a political canvasser—but only once had Lawrence happened to be watching when Will answered a knock and then, no doubt politely, sent the interloper away.

Oddly, no mean rumors circulated about the old man, no nasty teenage pranks were played on him. Rockvale was the respectful county seat. Over the years, Mr. Turley must have established himself so carefully, so consistently, that he had been accepted as he was and taken for an honest citizen. He had no church, did no charitable work, joined no men's lodge nor played a weekend sport. He had no known associates but lived as a cloistered monk alone in a cell, pursuing his meditative work in the world, and for that he was left somehow untouched.

But Lawrence and Nancy still could not understand how, for over fifty years, Will Turley had escaped persecution, even of the subtlest insidious sort. Last night before sleep, they had tried to reconstruct their conversations with him, and now over the charged-up voices of the sportscasters, Lawrence recalled a few of his phrases. "Words come at you, linger awhile, then fade off." Will had said something like that. "Imagine if you had to remember everything you once read!" That was the gist of it. They had all three agreed that a complete memory would be a terrifying burden, day upon day, month upon month, year upon year. "And yet, Will, all you must know—" Lawrence had begun to say, but the old man claimed that each moment was constantly being overwhelmed by the next. Lawrence still found it implausible that this man of seventy-some years had lived only as each moment flew by. What new moments could ever penetrate that solid brick house over there? The man must have lived entirely in the past. His books, whatever books they were, must have amounted to a huge encyclopedia of all past human knowledge.

The Hugginses themselves had a fair collection of reference books, histories and biographies, medical and financial texts, and the celebrated titles of African-American literature their daughter had given them, as well as their own mess of paperback bestsellers—mysteries and thrillers. And now that she was a graduate student, Chloe had assembled her own library up in Wisconsin of the African and Caribbean authors she was dissecting for her doctoral thesis.

Nancy had told her, when she called last night, that the old gentleman next door had died suddenly from a fall on the ice. Chloe had never even seen him, but she gasped at the news. "Oh, no, your sweet neighbor! He was your best pal down there. Oh, no! Poor guy, poor you!" But later in the call she had asked if they knew who was moving in next. The prospect of a new neighbor had not yet occurred to them, but naturally the house would be sold and Felipe, the Puerto Rican man who came to mow Will's lawn and clip the bushes in the summer, rake the leaves in the fall, and in the winter shovel the walks, would come no more.

By the time Nancy was driving home from the county hospital, the snow had stopped falling, and Felipe had indeed shoveled Will's walk and the path around back to the alley so the old man could drag out his trash barrel. Did he not know his employer was dead? Lawrence had not heard the shoveling because he had fallen asleep on the sofa during his third bowl game. But he had got himself up in time to clear their own walk before Nancy came in the kitchen door, stomping snow off her boots. The town plow was now rumbling down the alley, effacing the tracks of her tires.

AT THE BANK

O n Friday morning the second of January, Lawrence received a call from a law office in Riparian County. A Mr. Strite proposed to drive over that afternoon to discuss a particular aspect of the Turley estate and wondered if Dr. Nancy Huggins might possibly meet them as well. Lawrence was unsure of his wife's schedule but said he would call her beeper. "Does she really have to be here? She's a pediatrician, very busy after the holidays. I hope it isn't some dispute about the property line, some sort of easement we weren't informed of. Or is there something irregular in his account?" That Nancy was expected to attend caused fears to rise from Lawrence's usually calm interior. The lawyer said he would explain it all when he got there, and it turned out that Nancy could make time if she skipped lunch.

When they all met in Lawrence's office, Mr. Strite explained he was new on the job and until this week had been unacquainted with Mr. Turley's will. The original document had been drawn up decades ago by a Mr. Sturtevant, dead now for some years, but one year ago a Mr. Gaines, Strite's predecessor, had prepared the latest codicil. "I'm pretty much where you are with this thing," the young man said. He was glancing between the gray-templed, conservatively dressed large dark man sitting behind his polished desktop and his trim lighter-skinned wife with a lab coat peeking out beneath her winter parka. They sensed he had not expected them to be black. Mr. Strite adjusted his navy blue tie at the neck and opened a binder he had drawn from his briefcase. He seemed slightly nervous. "I'll summarize," he said and then began alternately reading and looking over at the Hugginses.

"'Upon his death'—William Riordan Turley's death, that is—'the property at 17 Phelps Street, Town of Rockvale, County of Sinnissippi, State of Illinois, and all its contents are to be offered free and clear'— which means with no tax implications, you understand, and no fees— 'to Lawrence and Nancy Huggins of 19 Phelps Street, Rockvale' et cetera, 'and any fees or taxes incurred are to'—well, come from the rest of the estate, blah blah blah—and it goes on about his cousin John Turley Lee's son, somewhere in Vermont, who is to inherit the revocable trust itself. Of course, you need not accept the property, in which case it reverts to the Turley estate and goes to the cousin's kid." Strite was now looking up at two astonished faces. "Perhaps you knew something of this?" But the Hugginses shook their heads. "So he never hinted at it?"

"I'm dumbfounded," said Lawrence at last. Nancy felt her tears coming again. The death had already shaken her, and now this amazing announcement! She wiped her blinking eyelids before any wetness could show.

"Don't ask me how or why this came about," said the lawyer. "I don't suppose Gaines knew much either. Let's just say he's no longer with the firm. But it's all right and properly drawn up. You'll probably want to think about it. The house and everything in it would be yours to dispose of as you wish. In a way it's kind of a responsibility, but it could also be profitable. On the way here, my GPS led me down Phelps Street. It's a nice-looking house, though yours at nineteen's in better condition. His trim needs fresh paint, and I suppose you'd want to update the kitchen and bath for resale. It's pretty much as is, let's just say."

"He was only our neighbor," Lawrence finally said. He was looking more closely at this slender young white man, no doubt recently out of law school, sent on this errand by the senior partners. "Mr. Strite?"

"Call me Rod," he said with an eager smile.

"Good, Rod, well, I don't know what to say yet. Or ask."

"He simply came to our house for suppers now and then," Nancy said.

"Not over a dozen times," added Lawrence.

"He seems to have been a tad eccentric," Rod Strite said. "So it's not been exactly a personal loss?"

"But we did like him very much," said Nancy.

"Tell us, Rod," said Lawrence, "do you have any notion why Mr. Turley retained lawyers over in Riparian County?"

"And an investment manager back in Chicago," Rod noted. "Apparently, he came out here years ago from the North Shore. Who knows!"

"Poor old Will," said Nancy, "he was full of secrets. We've never even been inside his house. No one seems to have. We don't know at all what we'd be accepting."

"I don't like the idea of gaining something from Will's death," said Lawrence. "And why us?"

"I'm new at this, Mr. Huggins," said Rod. "I've only just joined the firm. But in estate law, from all I studied in school, some pretty weird arrangements get made. Individuals aren't like governments having to be accountable to voters. Individuals can do some pretty crazy shit." Rod looked suddenly sheepish. "Not to speak ill of the dead," he quickly added.

"We barely knew him," said Nancy, "but we may be the only people he said more than two words to for years. We're told he kept to himself ever since coming here, when he was only twenty-one or -two."

"Well," said the young lawyer as he folded up Mr. Turley's last will and testament, "there's no immediate deadline. Probate may take some months, though the partners foresee no complications. The cousin's kid is getting plenty for himself, the lucky bum. Wish I had an eccentric relative. Doesn't sound like he ever even met the deceased. It's like a Victorian novel, isn't it?"

Nancy had some idea what he meant from watching *Masterpiece Theatre*, but to break the racial ice, Lawrence quipped, "Back then, I don't think we Hugginses would've stood much chance of having a long-lost rich uncle!"

The two men exchanged knowing laughs. Then Rod Strite placed his card on the desktop. "I'm glad it's the twenty-first century then, I guess," he said with a firm handshake for Lawrence and a gentler one for Nancy. He asked them to call him when they had decided what to do about their inheritance.

"But how will we know what it is we've accepted?" Nancy asked as they moved toward the office door. She must get back to the hospital, but this was all passing by too quickly.

"Unfortunately," said young Rod, "we'll still need permission to inspect the premises. An assessor will be appointed, the county auditor will have to clear all debts and affirm the deed, but we may be able to get you in for a look some time next week. Somebody has to be sure the pipes don't freeze, right?"

"What about the man who comes to shovel?" Lawrence wanted to know. They were out in the lobby now. The tellers' chat had ceased, and the loan officer was speaking low to a pair of clients.

"If you see him, have him give us a call. We want to make sure he's been paid."

"Tell you what," said Lawrence, "I'll keep him on. I'll pay him myself for both houses. I'm tired of doing my own shoveling. And I'll let him know that Mr. Turley is dead."

Around Town

On his Monday lunch hour, Lawrence ran into Felipe Reyes coming out of Freddy's Hardware. He conveyed the sad news and watched distress crease the small man's brow and then a grateful smile curl his lips when informed he now had two jobs on Phelps Street and from such a prominent employer. But suddenly a sharper dismay shrouded his pointy features. "I should have come over before to put sand and salt."

"You're not to blame, my friend," said Lawrence. "It was an accident. It was all in the way he happened to land."

"I did not see him maybe only the times he gives money instead of leaving envelope. I should have put sand and salt."

Lawrence grasped the trembling bare hand in his two gloved ones and shook it warmly. "It will come to us all, one last moment, and who knows when."

"Grace of God," said Felipe.

"Grace of God," echoed Lawrence, not letting go quite yet. "And I assure you, Mr. Turley didn't even know, he didn't regain consciousness."

Felipe appeared to find some comfort in that and promised to come when the next snow began to fall. Heading back to the bank, Lawrence considered how this little man from the islands had taken on the responsibility of clearing away a northern winter. Lawrence's own people had been in Chicago for generations and knew snow and ice as intimately as their untraceable ancestors had known the heat of Africa.

And now here he was in this little town of Rockvale with no more than three thousand inhabitants and maybe that many more out in the county. There was no Great Lake to put an edge to it but only twisty creeks and narrow streams flowing down to the muddy Sinnissippi. It felt claustrophobic with those limestone outcroppings along the bluffs by the meandering river. And such a small scale of things! The largest house in town was his own—and Will's. They had been built side by side in the 1870s for bank president Gregory Henshaw and Judge Elias Gale. Lawrence saw his tenancy of 19 Phelps Street as a sign of natural succession. Yet would he now prefer the judge's house? Over the weekend he had begun to think it might seem ungrateful to wait until he and Nancy had inspected the premises before accepting the bequest. Whatever shape the house was in, it would not incur any financial loss. They could collect rent or sell it and, even in these uncertain times, come out ahead. They had certainly been left something valuable by the good old man.

But Nancy had another concern. How might it be viewed around town that they, of all people, had been given outright one of the finest residences in the county? They had not lived beside William Turley for over five decades, they had not remained respectful of his solitude for all those years. They had materialized from the city a mere two years ago and presumed to invite the town hermit to supper. If anyone else had ever made such a gesture, nothing had come of it, so what was so deserving about these black Hugginses? Lawrence suggested they consult Susie Gitchell, with whom Nancy had a cordial, if somewhat formal, acquaintanceship.

Monday after work, she caught Susie at the top of the library steps locking up. The old Carnegie building was her true home. Susie said she ought to retire right now but could never quite bring herself to do so. "And so my big old girlhood mystery man is gone now," she said taking Nancy's arm instead of the iron railing.

"It's so sad," said Nancy.

"When I was a girl," said Susie safely on the well-shoveled sidewalk, "he was something of a Heathcliff, so romantic and mysterious. I was eleven or twelve. He was ten years older than me. The *Gazette* said he died at seventy-six. I was already quite the reader then. I doubt if I'd yet made it through *Wuthering Heights*, but I'd seen the movie at the old Star."

"Ralph Fiennes," Nancy said, pronouncing the L.

"I mean the old movie, dear," said Susie. "Merle Oberon and Laurence Olivier." She was staring up at the pale glass globe of a streetlamp. "I think it was William Turley and his books that turned me into a librarian. Back then, I worked here on Saturdays. And to think, just a month ago he came in to use a computer! He was still sending away for odd volumes in his collection. I'd taught him how to search the Internet. It was the most we ever conversed up close, but all he'd say was 'How?' or 'I see.' If I tried to interest him in something from the new books, he'd say he didn't read living authors. But, Nancy, somehow you and your husband had him in for supper? People around town couldn't believe it."

They were proceeding slowly down the block. "I hope they didn't hold it against us," said Nancy.

Susie grasped her wrist tighter. "But why would they?"

"I mean, why us?"

"No, it seemed rather wonderful," said the librarian.

"But we're—newcomers." Nancy left it at that, then she assured Susie that everyone had been very welcoming.

The librarian's sagging cheeks puffed out with some concern. "I'm glad you haven't chanced on the more small-minded people," she said and continued slowly down the sidewalk.

"I wonder," said Nancy, having decided to test it out, "how it might be viewed if somehow Lawrence and I managed to acquire his house."

"William Turley's?"

"We've been told by his lawyer that it's an option we may have."

"You already own the Henshaw house, which is every bit as grand. I grew up across the street in the yellow bungalow under an old maple that's now just the stump. Mrs. Henshaw was still alive when Mr. Turley bought the Gale house. I don't suppose it's worth what it used to be. But would you mean to own them both?"

"It's only something we're contemplating." They were now at the corner where Nancy had parked her station wagon. "May I give you a lift, Mrs. Gitchell?"

"I always walk, but thank you. Does it worry you, living next to that empty old house now? Is that it? I doubt anyone else would want it. They all want to build out past the hospital in those additions. Who wants an old drafty house?"

"We wouldn't be resented?" Nancy asked. "We wonder, as outsiders—"

Susie Gitchell cast a stern glance from Nancy's little knit hat down to her shiny black leather boots. "Some people might only think you were fools," she said.

When she drove home, Nancy pondered those words. Susie felt they would be wasting their money, but of course that was not the actual issue. Free though it might be, it was still a somewhat derelict property. Yet would it be more foolish to refuse the gift for fear of being thought fools?

At the supper table, Nancy told Lawrence it might be wisest to leave the house to the cousin in Vermont. How much longer would they be staying in Rockvale anyway?

In fact, people in town were already speculating about what would happen to the dead man's house. Perhaps it was in homage to the old widow Gale that no one had ever thrown stones at William Turley's windows or toilet-papered his trees or yelled crude things at him when he walked through town. Children avoided his door on Beggars' Night, not for fear of a creepy old man from some horror movie, but because even the children sensed something honorable in the judge's house, as if it were the home of a disabled war veteran. And after the widely reported sight of old Turley being ushered in the front door of the wealthy black couple next door, the man himself may even have gained in honor. Something more marvelous was occurring behind the closed doors of bank president Henshaw's house than the townsfolk could quite imagine. Even the small-minded ones would say, "I hear the old gent went visiting next door where those colored people live." It was a strange alliance no one could comprehend.

The tellers never did ask their boss what he had learned from those visits with the town's recluse. Mr. Turley had continued to shuffle in to cash his checks. "You know, now that we're all AmTrust, you could switch your account over here," Millie Stover told him once, "and anyway, you can use your ATM card at either branch." But she had only received a shake of his gray head. Because he was a big man, as tall as Lawrence Huggins and as broad, if no longer as solid, he garnered more respect than had he been small like Felipe Reyes, who went about practically unnoticed, tending lawns and shoveling snow, as if he did not quite exist. William Turley performed no apparent function at all, yet he was an essential presence in the town of Rockvale, Illinois.

Tuesday afternoon, Lawrence was scanning the drugstore shelves for toiletries and overheard a conversation at the soda fountain in back.

"It won't be the same," Joe Etnyre, the postman, said to Gerry Waite, the electrician. "No more old geezer walking by, all genial and quiet. You didn't ever talk to him?"

"Whoever did?" said Gerry. "He sure weren't talking when Henry picked him up off the ice and drug him into his truck. Now Henry thinks he should've called the police first, but the poor old guy was still breathing then. Henry was in some kind of panic, I guess."

"He did the right thing," Joe said.

"Henry told me he didn't even stop to think. He's all messed up about it still."

"No, he did right, Gerry. No time to lose," said the postman.

"He'd come in here for his prescriptions," said Mr. Doyle, the pharmacist, who had walked back to the soda fountain to fix himself a black cow. "I won't tell you precisely what they were for, but there was nothing much wrong with him aside from the normal aches and pains."

"And he never said a thing, did he?" said Joe Etnyre.

"He'd just hand me the 'scrip."

In small towns, it is usual to stop and say a few words to anyone you halfway know, and you may say hello even to those you don't. In Chicago, Lawrence had no such leisure, too many pedestrians, too much to get done. But by now he had revived the habit of sidewalk chat from his childhood street corner because out here people actually wanted to talk to him, to be seen talking to him in particular, as if to demonstrate how they personally knew the black bank manager. And naturally, the mothers of her patients had plenty to say to Nancy. Folks from the Methodist church would stop and talk, even those the Hugginses had never been introduced to. It might have seemed a bit forced at first, but Nancy and Lawrence decided to credit it at face value.

So now he stepped up to the counter with his purchases and said, "Hi there, men, yes, it's quite a sad thing. Our next door neighbor, as you know."

"That's what I read in the paper," said Gerry Waite. "That was nice, what you said."

"After I delivered to Mr. Huggins's house," said Joe, "I'd go all the way back to the sidewalk and skip Mr. Turley's, because he kept a P.O. box and I didn't want to walk across his lawn to number fifteen and maybe disturb him."

"We were all considerate of his privacy," said Mr. Doyle. "But I hear you had him in for supper some evenings, Mr. Huggins."

This was the first open mention Lawrence had ever heard of what was common knowledge in town. He did not care to claim a special privilege, so he said, "Nancy invited him after we moved in. We didn't realize he was so solitary."

"But he came," Mr. Doyle said. "I don't mean to pry—"

"He never said much of a personal nature, that's the thing," said Lawrence. "He was always polite and sure enjoyed my wife's cooking. Mostly he'd talk ideas."

"You said in the paper he was real educated," Gerry said.

"I don't know that he ever went to college," said Lawrence. "He just read lots of books."

"That's one way to get an education," said Gerry. "Cheaper, too."

The four of them chuckled and nodded, and then Mr. Doyle sighed and carried his black cow to the cash register so he could ring up Lawrence's toothpaste and dental floss and mouthwash and deodorant.

THE JUDGE'S HOUSE

Chloe had visited at Christmas but preferred to spend the rest of her break in Chicago with friends and use the libraries. Deet was coming down to see some theater. Her parents knew there was little for Chloe to do amongst the perfectly nice white strangers of their new small world, so they did not expect her to stay long. Besides, she would come down again in the spring. But Nancy and Lawrence had agreed to consult her now about their surprising inheritance. In due course, Chloe would have a right to it, not that she would ever move to Rockvale, not that her parents would remain there much longer, but property always had some value.

"What shall we tell her?" Nancy asked, holding out the phone with a finger pointed to speed-dial Chloe's cell.

"That we don't know what we're going to do yet." Lawrence was leaning against the arched doorway to the living room. "We'll just say we've been offered the house free and clear and see what she says."

"But we shouldn't put it all on her," said Nancy.

"She'll want to know what's the catch," Lawrence predicted.

"You do it, honey, you'll be more business-like." Nancy retracted her finger but did not yet pass the phone because her husband was now gazing out the bay window into the darkness next door. It's sitting over there, he was telling himself, on its snowy lot with its dark evergreens, and not even the streetlamp hints that it's there, empty and cold. He yearned to go over and turn up the heat.

"She'll worry about the expense it might entail," said Nancy. "You can reassure her. She thinks I'm impulsive."

"You mean if we accept."

"Either way," Nancy said and went to sit on the sofa clutching her hands in her lap.

Lawrence punched the number and soon heard a commotion on the other end. "What are we interrupting, sweetie?" he asked. Chloe must be out in a crowd of Chicagoans.

"We're almost at the theater. It's Shakespeare, but with an all-black cast. Deet knows some of them. He says it'll be nasty."

"Deet's not much into uplift," joked her father.

"So, Dads, what are you two up to out there in the sticks?"

"This probably isn't a good time to talk. Nothing special. We'll reach you tomorrow."

"No, I can hear you fine."

"It sounds like a party back there."

"We just got into the lobby. It's cold outside. Now Deet's glasses are all fogging up. He can't even see me."

"Seriously, sweetie, we'll call tomorrow."

"I can't see his eyes. He looks like a zombie!"

"We just wanted a nice long talk with our girl."

"Tomorrow then. You got it," said Chloe. "But, hey, not too early."

"Ask where she's staying," Nancy whispered.

"You with your cousins still?" Lawrence asked loud enough to be heard over the theatergoers.

"And everybody here's totally fine," said Chloe. "Don't worry."

"Tell them we miss them all," said Lawrence. Then it was too hard to hear, so he clicked off. "At least we have one more day to think this through," he told his wife.

But she did not want to think it through any further. She had suddenly determined that they must take the house. It was no longer the town's resentment that she feared, but the idea that they were being deprived of something, for whatever reason, rightfully theirs. She had the sudden strange notion that they had earned the house with her home cooking and Lawrence's patient way of letting Will eat his supper in peace, awaiting the moment when a thought came to his mind and, between bites, he would put it into words. Nancy herself had a harder time with silence. With anxious mothers, she kept up the comforting chat during their kids' checkups, all the more so when there was something to be really concerned about.

"It might be better to present it to Chloe as an accomplished fact," Lawrence said. "I wish we knew for sure what to do."

"We'll accept."

"We will? You've decided?" Nancy patted the cushion beside her, and he sat down slowly with a twist to his lower lip indicating doubt. "Still, if we decline," he said, "the town wouldn't ever have to know. The Vermont cousin would put it up for sale. Nothing about us would need to change."

"But it's ours," said Nancy reaching over to pinch Lawrence's cheek away from the dark bay window behind them.

"Technically, it's still in probate," he said. "The cousin may even contest it."

"Rod Strite seemed to think not. The cousin never knew Will."

Lawrence saw how this was the truest point for Nancy. His work managed mere funds, but hers managed the health of small living bodies. He thought of the house next door only as a property, but to Nancy it was a gift from a human being. "But why us?" he asked, the question they were both growing weary of.

The next day, a nurse named Elsie Stover, mother of Millie who worked at the bank, asked Nancy if she and her husband were thinking of restoring the judge's house the way those retired city folk were doing down in Sandport on the Mississippi. "It wouldn't pay off in a burg like this," she cautioned, "what with so many of us leaving town and businesses closing. Even our hospital's affiliated with somewheres else." She swept her hand out as if to display the long pea-green corridor down which they were walking. "And the Chicago bank took over our bank. But I'm glad," she added, "because it brought you and Mr. Huggins. You think there's more city folk wanting to move out here, I mean nice ones like you, you know, to get away from all the crime? But what would they ever do here in Rockvale?"

"There always has to be a bank," Nancy reassured her. "There'll always be a public library. There has to be a courthouse. We'll always be a county, Elsie." Nancy had surprised herself with the *we*.

"I don't know," said the nurse. "When I was young, Phelps Street was where the rich lived. Does Mr. Huggins think there's anyone but him who could buy there now?"

"You heard that? It was only a passing thought I shared with Susie Gitchell," said Nancy. "Did she assume it was a done deal?"

"She said something about it to my daughter," Elsie said.

Word had also come to Henry Settle, from his old schoolmate Millie Stover, of what was up with the judge's house. They were grabbing a quick lunch at the Greek's—a grilled cheese and tomato for her, gyros for him, and plenty of coffee—when her boss came in for a salad and a slice to go. Lawrence heard Henry say, "Thing is, someone's got to care for the place. Pipes could bust."

"They shut off the pipes," Millie said. "The lawyer sent the real estate people over. Oh, hi, Mr. Huggins. We were talking about Mr. Turley's house."

"Yes, they're seeing to everything," said Lawrence.

"He was a hottie, that lawyer," said Millie.

"I'm seriously jealous," Henry said.

He got a nudge from her elbow, and Kostas behind the counter said, "If you two don't start going out together soon, you never will."

So they ate in silence while Kostas made up the salad. Then Millie said, "You doing better now, Henry—no jitters?"

"I get freaked easy," he said. "I'm not too good at seeing blood. He was a heavy old sucker too. I suppose I'm the only one in town who ever actually touched him."

"But you mustn't feel bad for all you tried to help," said Lawrence.

"Man, you're the hero," said Kostas. "You're legend now."

Henry licked at the tzatziki sauce sticking to his fingers and glanced at Millie. Lawrence could see how much he liked her, but on one quiet afternoon at the bank she had told him that Henry Settle would always only be a friend. And now she said she had to go back to work. "Right, Mr. Huggins?"

But Lawrence, with styrofoam boxes in a plastic sack, stopped first at the post office, curious to see if they had received word of where to send the mail from William Turley's box.

"I'm to forward it to Stark, Weber, Brennheim, and Braun," said Eddie Boyce. "That's his lawyers. There's only one padded mailer now containing, no doubt, some other old book. I'm used to his packages. This one's light. Check it out." He balanced it on his palm like a little pillow. "How did old Turley ever read so many books, Mr. Huggins?

Maybe he never actually read them. Maybe he just liked collecting them. There's people like that who want everything in a given category, the complete this or that, just to have it and keep it all in order on shelves or in drawers or in the attic. Like I had a stamp collection the old postmistress got me started on when I was a kid. But in a post office, everything comes in and goes right out again. Albeit in a neat orderly fashion," he added.

That night, the time came again to call Chloe. Lawrence had reached some conclusions. If Nancy wanted the house, they would accept it and decide afterward what to do with it. They need not explain it to their fellow townspeople. Did it matter? The house would be legally theirs. So far, they had no idea what was inside it other than books. There might be treasures. All the contents as is, Strite had said. If it's nothing we want, we'll have a garage sale. Lawrence did not feel greedy so much as curious. It was the only way to solve the mystery of their neighbor's reclusive life. If they declined his gift, they would never know anything further. The house would sit there, taunting them for having been too fearful to take it on. But we won't stay in this town, Lawrence reminded himself, I'll be reassigned to Chicago, maybe to a suburb, I'm fifty-three, they're bound to reward me for handling this branch so well. Then again, he thought, it's not a great year for banks— maybe I'll be put out to pasture. He had to laugh at himself.

But they had always lived uncertainly. When he and Nancy started out nearly thirty years ago, what safe place could a young black couple be assured of in this country? He had helped her through med school, stuck to his desk, come up on his merits. Chicago Title had already merged with Marquette and then AmTrust absorbed it all, and he kept coming up. They were finally ready for men who looked like him. Lawrence had almost forgotten what it once felt like in Chicago, that flicker of a client's eyelid when registering his color. It was only here in Sinnissippi County that those old awkward split-seconds recurred.

Nancy had noticed as well, during their first weeks before word had spread of the new doctor, the new banker, those subtle twitches at the corners of mouths, those quick readjustments in tones of voice. These people were ready enough for a female pediatrician, even preferred one after the old-school male retired, but there came a perceptible hesitation before the handshake that never happened anymore in

Chicago, that flicker, that twitch before the over-polite greeting. And then soon, the unruffled child would be traipsing happily back out to the waiting room with a smile and a stuffed animal.

"So we're agreed," Lawrence announced when he set the roast chicken on the table. He had picked it up from the rotisserie case at the IGA on his way home.

"I still want you to do the explaining," said Nancy.

It did not take much. Chloe was so high on showing Deet off to her city cousins, and the play had been amazing, especially hanging out afterward with Deet's actor friends, that she could countenance just about anything. "It's you guys' life," she said. "You're not checking out anytime soon, I trust. If it was me, I'd cash it in now, but hey."

"We may yet," said Lawrence, "cash it in, I mean. But we want first to honor the old gentleman's kindness."

"There was a line in the play last night," Chloe said, "that if you want human kindness, get yourself a dog."

"Sounds like your sophisticated Deet," said her father.

"No, Dads, in the play, by Shakespeare! You two can have the kind old man's house if you want. What do you mean by *honoring* though?"

"Your mother feels we shouldn't turn down a gift."

"Don't put it all on me," yelled Nancy from across the room so Chloe would hear.

"No, we've both agreed, but we don't know why he left it to us, sweetie. We don't quite know how to think about it."

Nancy could not resist taking the phone now, so she strode over and grabbed it. "Chloe, it's a lovely old home, the judge's house, built right after the Civil War. The brick one, remember? We might even move over there, if we like it more, and then rent out this one. All it needs is some fresh paint on the trim."

"No, Moms, it's totally great. But how come I never once even saw your old Mr. Turley? You never had him over when I was there. If he was such a kind gentleman, he might've wanted to meet your promising intellectual daughter!"

"He wouldn't have wanted to impose on our brief family time."

"Hey," Chloe said, "maybe his gift was to rectify past wrongs, a one-man reparation sort of thing."

"Maybe he just took kindly to us," said Nancy.

"You want to speak to Cousin Trudy now? She's right here breathing on my neck."

"You hush now," Nancy heard Trudy say.

After Lawrence had taken the phone back and explained it all again to his old cousin, Gertrude Huggins, who raised him, the fact of their having inherited 17 Phelps Street finally began to settle in his mind. Tomorrow he would call the lawyer, and then surely the news would start spreading fast around town.

AT THE OTHER BANK

"'ll set the wheels rolling," said the enthusiastic voice into his ear. "Congratulations, Mr. Huggins."

"I suppose I'm to be congratulated," said Lawrence. He was alone in his office with the door closed. He seldom closed the door, because he wanted the tellers and officers out there to see him hard at work and yet know they could talk to him whenever they needed to, but he had not wanted anyone to overhear this conversation. "So what comes next?" he asked the young lawyer.

"Probate first, then the paperwork. I'll have it all drawn up, Ryleston Properties will do the transfer. That'll only take a couple thousand from the estate. Mr. Turley wanted all transactions done over here in Riparian County. He sure had a thing about keeping his business out of Rockvale. Still, your own court has to do the probate because he lived in Sinnissippi. Mr. Ryleston thinks he can get you and your wife in next week for a look."

Lawrence said he understood somebody had already gone to check on the water pipes.

"And do the inspection, evaluate the contents, assess the whole deal actually. Probate needs all that in order to settle the estate, pay off outstanding debts, that sort of stuff. I haven't yet seen the report, but you don't need to concern yourself, Mr. Huggins. It's all coming to you and the good doctor, no hassle. That's what I'm here for. When I hear the partners talk about abuse cases and felonies, I'm glad to be in estates. Except I'm sure I'll find they can get weird too."

Lawrence was letting Rod Strite talk away. It was not on his dime. Lawrence had worked for everything he got, and so had Nancy. It had never occurred to them that one day they would somehow get lucky, if luck was what this was. Last night when they lay in bed, Nancy started speculating about the furnishings and decor of their new house, but Lawrence said once they got inside they were bound to be disappointed, maybe even appalled—and sad for lonesome old Will. Better not to predict. Nancy nuzzled up under his arm and promised to stop fantasizing. She admitted she had even tried to go peek in the windows but couldn't see through the drawn curtains anyway.

But Lawrence decided to make his own preliminary investigation, not of the house but of Mr. Turley's account. He had access to the system for the current figures but wanted the whole history, so he made an appointment to meet his counterpart at AmTrust-Riparian. The next morning, he drove to the neighboring county seat to the three-story glass-fronted new building with ample parking in its perfectly plowed lot. It was a larger operation than his. This county had six times the population of Sinnissippi plus a college and the old barge town where ex-urbanites were restoring fine old homes like his—his two he had to remind himself. Were he and Nancy ex-urbanites? The term did not sit well with Lawrence. In bad old times, Hugginses were country folk, but for generations they had been Chicagoans, and so had Nancy's people, the Sublettes. Chloe had so much city in her blood that she would surely land some urban position with her degree and drag Deet along with her, if she had her way.

Lawrence pulled into a convenient space near the entrance. Today, he had left his Civic with Nancy and, for the snowy roads, driven her Forester. When they moved he had invested in an all-wheel-drive wagon because he did not want his wife stuck in some backwoods ditch on a dark night.

Approaching the bank's plate-glass doors, Lawrence noted AmTrust's new logo stenciled there in sky blue. The big redesign had not yet reached his branch. Only two years ago, the AmTrust name had arrived out here in dark blue block letters, and these stylish new italics did not inspire the same confidence. But now his branch would look outmoded until the new stencils and signage were delivered.

"Mr. Higgins?" inquired the receptionist. Lawrence ignored her mistake as well as her directions to the elevator and opted for the carpeted stairs. Soon he found himself in the third-floor office of Rose Carron, whom he had met at the Labor Day retreat for regional managers and their families. AmTrust had rented a conference center set on a bluff above the Sinnissippi. There were games for the kids and a swimming pool, and Nancy had strolled about the grounds with Rose's husband while the small Carrons swam and tossed horseshoes and all the managers participated in seminars inside what had once been the country house of a wealthy Chicagoan.

"It's been too long," Rose said, "and Alexander adored your wife. We should all get together again soon."

"Yes, let's. Great photo," Lawrence said pointing to the three little blonds framed on her desk.

"They had a blast, but I don't know why the bank thinks a retreat's how we prefer to spend our holiday weekend. Have a seat. And your daughter's in grad school up in Madison?"

"Appleton," said Lawrence. "Lawrence University. She chose it for the name." He was sure he had made the same quip back in September.

"Of course! And she's getting her doctorate? I dread the cost when mine reach college."

"Chloe's fully funded," said Lawrence but added, so Rose would not assume it was only for diversity, "She's the brains of the family. She's writing on Anglophone literature of the African diaspora, which is beyond me."

"I was a plain business major," said Rose.

"As was I."

They smiled sympathetically, and Lawrence felt ready to explain his visit. He assumed a serious expression and was about to begin when Rose said, "So you're here on a personal matter?"

"Not bank business, however—" He breathed in deep. "Well, it has its financial aspect." And so he told the story of William Turley's bequest, attempting to sound as baffled by it as Rose appeared to be, but in the telling, it actually started making curious sense to him. The old man had no close family, had no friends in the town or anywhere else, had no charitable interests as far as Lawrence knew, had only the Hugginses' neighborly presence. In over fifty years, Will had spoken more words to them than to all the rest of humanity, though he had apparently read his books aloud to the four walls of his empty house, each word sounding in the air then vanishing to be replaced by the next.

But aside from a "how-de-do" on the sidewalk, the only words any human ear received from William Turley were those addressed to Nancy and Lawrence Huggins, his heirs—well, aside from the cousin who would inherit the trust fund. But that the house and all it contained would come to his hosts of a mere dozen suppers somehow did make sense now.

"Unbelievable! I'm bewildered," said Rose. "You and your wife must've brought the old goat some happiness."

"What we did was rather minimal," Lawrence said.

Rose Carron was wearing a dapper charcoal gray pantsuit and beige blouse with a turquoise necklace. Lawrence guessed she was not yet forty and here she was, managing this large branch with its gleaming new building. She had been coaxed out from her North Shore suburb, Winnetka, as he remembered. It was a promotion, but now her kids' schools were not nearly as good and her husband had to give up Northwestern for Knighton College. Alexander Carron was some sort of dean, he remembered. But you could live more cheaply out here, you could live quite well. The Hugginses could never afford a house like 19 Phelps Street in the village of Winnetka, let alone two.

"What seemed minimal to you may not have been minimal to him," Rose said. "Maybe you were the nicest people in his life. Oldsters get lonesome."

"But there must've once been someone nicer. He once had family, must've had friends."

"You mentioned the cousin, and I—"

"That was what I was coming to," Lawrence interrupted her and resumed the professional tone he had let slip while he told his tale. He must keep a cool head, so he would not appear as vulnerable as he suddenly felt. He realized he had a deep-buried fear that some mean trick might still be played on them by the laws of inheritance. There was the white cousin in Vermont. Rod Strite had casually dismissed his claim, but Rod was fresh out of law school. Why would that cousin not want the hundred thousand a sale of the house might bring?

"You're wondering about the revocable trust—" Rose began.

"Well—" He did not want to seem overly inquisitive. He felt sweat beading on his upper lip and brow. "If I may be direct, Rose." She seemed a bit nervous too. The last thing he wanted was to make an inappropriate request of a fellow manager.

"You're wondering how much loot William Turley had," Rose said.

"But here's my concern," Lawrence began again, relieved to see a twinkle in her eye. "The estate will pay the upfront expenses, and I've seen the considerable balance he left in checking, some twenty thousand actually. I can't imagine why he kept such an amount in cash, but if that's all there is and the transaction whittles it down and the Vermont cousin only gets ten or twelve thousand—"

"He'll contest it? I don't think so, Lawrence, unless he's a greedy little pig. Look, Bell Investments in Chicago has been in touch. I would've stopped you sooner, if you weren't telling such a good story. Of course, we didn't know about the house, that it was to be yours or even that you lived next door to the old goat—that's what Mr. Bell calls him—but we hold the trust here. Some time back in the 1950s, Mr. Turley was left the life insurance payout of a soldier killed over in Korea." Rose now swiveled to face her computer desk and quickly pulled up a file. "We don't know the reason why—maybe Mr. Bell does. I never asked. The lawyer who set it all up died awhile back. Anyway, the money wasn't from family—no, it was, let's see, from Private Caleb Pitchley—Pitchley, Turley! Funny. Mr. Turley came into the money on August 13, 1954, when he turned twenty-one. Our Mr. Bell's father was his man in Chicago back then. The relationship with us—with the old Riparian County Bank, I should say—began some months later when Turley moved out here. His lawyer was, let's see, a Mr. Sturtevant in the little town of Josephine, west of here. All very discrete, in the sense of *separate*. Did you know that *discreet* with the Es together means *private* but *discrete* with the T in between means *separate*? I learned that from my son Oliver, who's in sixth grade. So Turley bought the house over in Rockvale, and ever since we've been holding the trust and paying out his insurance and taxes and utilities and anything else that's come up. We don't go back that far electronically, probably won't ever bother. Would you like to see the print file?"

"No, no, I was only concerned there might have been something behind all this we didn't know about," Lawrence said.

"I'm sure there was plenty behind it at the time," said Rose, "but I doubt we'll ever know what it was. This wet-behind-the-ears lawyer's been straightening it out with us. We hate to lose a trust of this size, but the cousin will probably move it to some bank in—where was it, Goshen, Vermont. He'd be wise to keep Mr. Bell, though. This John Lee the Third, the son of Turley's first cousin of the same name—young Strite says he's a back-to-the-lander, makes his own maple syrup and raises sheep and spins the wool, the whole romantic scenario. Old hippie from the nineteen seventies. He'll probably want to sink the money in a wind farm or solar panels or some sustainability thing. Anyway, the house in Rockvale's small potatoes to him. The trust is worth, last count—let's see, one point three million."

"A life insurance policy amounted to—"

"Remember, Lawrence, it was nineteen fifty-four, and the Mr. Bells, father and son, knew what they were doing. Not that old Turley cared. No matter what this new year brings, and it ain't gonna be great, though we're not supposed to say so, the Vermont cousin will be just fine." With another twinkle she added, "I wouldn't feel too bad, Lawrence, about depriving the distant relative. He's getting what matters to normal people. What you're getting, as far as I can see, is what mattered to Mr. Turley."

At the Hospital

ancy had an hour before her next appointment. Usually, she would go over her records to refamiliarize herself with upcoming patients. She liked to remember which girl had read all the Harry Potters and which boy's dad let him play Grand Theft Auto, who had a big brother on the high school basketball team, who liked which Jonas brother. For the moms, she was up on what their husbands did and if they loved living in that new addition out a country road or were still raising chickens. Nancy was more at ease with people than her husband was. She remembered people whole. All it took was a quick review and they would snap into focus. Lawrence was a facts-and-figures man, much as he liked people and wanted to be liked. Nancy was confident she was liked, even out here in this alien world. She recognized the fact that, for these folk, bright teeth in a dark face made smiles all the friendlier. Her little patients loved Dr. Nancy, Elsie Stover had told her. Having only produced one Chloe, Nancy by now had acquired dozens of supplemental, but thankfully temporary, offspring.

Dorie Gault was the next appointment. The note read: "Squirt gun, checkered apron." Dorie's mother let her wear it because Dorie wanted to be a waitress, and the squirt gun was for rude customers. But rather than review her files, Nancy decided to stroll down the corridor to Dr. Pratt's office hoping to find him unengaged, as he often was at the end of the day. He was the one who had admitted the dying William Turley and witnessed his last breath.

"Nancy!" said Dr. Pratt—Artie, as he wished to be called.

"I'm not interrupting?"

"Come in! I hear you and the banker are coming up in the world."

"Is that what it is?"

"I hear you're taking on a white elephant. I'm not sure I'd want it myself. Our new place outside of town is tight as a drum and no more steps to climb. Etta doesn't feature another hip replacement. And now we've got central air and humidifiers and dehumidifiers and a trash compacter and a wood-burning stove in the den."

"When did you hear about the judge's house, Artie?"

"It's all over town. Susie Gitchell told me first."

"She thinks we're fools to take it on. We haven't even been inside yet."

"Whoever has? And the real estate people aren't talking. I'd expected them to get Henry Settle to check on things. He's the boy who found the old fella. They should give Henry a break. He needs the work. But they've got their own people. We'll be glad when it's our own folks in there again. You planning to move over and sell the Henshaw house or what?"

"We haven't planned. It's still a mystery what we've come into."

Artie leaned back in his chair with a satisfied grin. "So the rumor's true! The old fella left it to you! I say *old fella*, but he wasn't much older than me. I remember when he came to town in fifty-four. I was in high school, and this big broad young man from Chicago plunks himself down in that house after Judge Gale's widow went to the nursing home. And except for Mr. Settle, the father, doing some carpentering, no one's been inside since. Will Turley used to work outside in his garden in the early days. I'd been hoping to make friends, but he didn't have much to say. I'd saunter by and say hello and compliment him on his irises or daffodils or whatever was blooming, and he'd say 'how-de-do' but look over for only a split second. We all gave up pretty soon. Strange to say, Nancy, no one took a dislike to young Will, nor did they after we all got older. He had his secrets, as I now know. After medical school, I came back home to practice, and he was still here, off to the post office and the stores and nodding politely, the way he'd do, but striding right along. Maybe he once took books out of the library, but Susie says ever since she's been librarian, which is well over forty years, he never took out a book because he had his own at home. Seems he had a thing about owning them. You're going to have a cartload to dispose of, Nancy. You've got yourselves a pig in a poke."

"Maybe they're valuable," Nancy said.

Artie made a doubtful laugh and then said, "But see, I treated Will a few times." And the old doctor's expression turned solemn. "Just minor ailments, aches and pains, he'd say. I wrote out prescriptions. He never came in for a proper checkup. He wouldn't take off his clothes, and I wasn't about to insist. Besides, I don't think he was ill a single day in his life. But his aches and pains—just wanted some painkillers, some relaxants. So I'm going to tell you something now, Nancy. It's between us, professionally, and you mustn't let it out around town. Naturally, I had to attend to the corpse before the funeral home swept him off to Riparian County. Why couldn't he be kept here at Frank's until cremation? But somehow, the home over there had arrangements in place, and even Frank knew about it. Will Turley didn't even want his dead body laid out here in Rockvale! And maybe I know why."

"He was a very private man," said Nancy.

"Yes, but there's a reason only I know," said Artie Pratt. Some enjoyment was showing through his thin-lipped grimace. "I haven't even told Etta, she's too sensitive. You see, all over Will Turley's chest and back were dozens of ancient scars, as if from the lash of a whip— deep cuts, bad ones, Nancy, that healed slow. They must've been inflicted in his youth when his flesh was tender. They did heal up, but there they were, still plain to see, hadn't gone away in all these years. He was marked for life. But nothing on his buttocks, which were smooth as a baby's."

Nancy's stomach had turned in on itself. She felt herself collapsing from inside. She had just remembered the scars of a runaway slave in a movie she had seen as a girl. She had been to the matinee with her girlfriends and come straight home and run right to her room and put her head under the pillow, and her mother came in and said, "Darling, what happened? You're shaking something terrible." But Nancy would not tell her mother what she had seen.

AT THE POST OFFICE

Still stunned after learning the amount of the Turley trust, Lawrence stopped at the Riparian mall for a burger and found a card to thank Cousin Trudy for taking care of Chloe and, presumably, Deet. Under the word *thanks* the cover showed a clean and orderly domestic scene, but on the inside, where it said "for making us feel at home," the lampshades and paintings were cocked sideways, a beer can had spilled on the coffee table and was dripping onto the carpet, the sofa cushions lay askew, and dirty clothes were tossed and draped about. Lawrence crossed out the "us" and wrote in "them" and signed it, "Love, Cousin Lawr." But he knew Chloe had been a most helpful guest and assumed Deet had behaved himself.

He pulled the Forester up behind the bank but decided first to go over to the post office down the block and buy stamps. It was an excuse to see what else Eddie Boyce might say about the comings and goings from Will's post box.

"Forwarded any more packages to the lawyers, Eddie?" he asked offhandedly as he peeled a Liberty Bell *forever* stamp from the little book and stuck it on the bright yellow envelope.

"Somebody's birthday?" Eddie asked.

"Just a thank-you card."

"My mom taught me always to write thank-you's," Eddie said. "No, I presume that was the last package, unless he's still ordering from that great Internet in the sky."

"That's where they keep the Internet, Eddie," Lawrence said with a wink.

"So we're told," said Eddie, "so we're told. You know, Mr. Huggins, the books he ordered came from all over the world. Once—I shouldn't admit it, but in confidence I'll tell you—one of those packages came in unsealed. Maybe it was by Homeland Security? So I took a peek. It was from a bookstore in Australia! A town called Toowoomba. I Google-Earthed it. It's about as far away as anything's ever come from in my ten years on the job. There were two big red books and two small blue ones. I believe they were missing volumes from his sets. I wrote myself a note." Eddie took his wallet from his back pocket and drew out a wrinkled slip of paper. "I don't know why I carry this around, but it was the only clue I had to the old man since he'd just nod when I'd say, 'More books for you, Mr. Turley.' The big red books were, see, from the novels of Honoré—you pronounce the E because of the accent mark—de Balzac, *The Petty Bourgeois*, Volume One and Volume Two. They had illustrations with tissue paper liners, and some pages weren't even cut apart. No one could ever have read those books straight through. The little blue ones were a quarter the size, but they'd definitely been read because some Australian had underlined here and there and torn off thin strips from the margins now and again to mark their place, I suppose. It was Volumes One and Two—see, I wrote it all down—of *Is He Popenjoy?* by Anthony Trollope. Now, without the E that would mean 'whore' in common parlance. And what's *popenjoy*? I've heard of a popinjay, it's a kind of bird. Anyway, it was from the World's Classics edition. See what I mean about Mr. Turley's collecting? Now the question is if he read them himself once he got them or just put them in alphabetical order on a shelf. You could tell now if you located those red books and found if the pages were cut. Is it true you're maybe going to buy the place, Mr. Huggins? That's the word around town."

All this time, Lawrence had been carefully attending while trying to appear only vaguely interested.

"You won't tell anyone I snooped, will you?"

"Of course not, Eddie, but I'll tell you something in return, if you'll promise not to tell either." Lawrence did not know why he was about to do this. He stopped himself to look the skinny, curly-haired redhead in the eyes. Eddie raised his right hand to solemnly swear. "We're not actually buying it," Lawrence said. He let the pronouncement register in Eddie's widening blue eyes. "But," he said and paused again for the fun of it—he had no idea why he felt compelled to go on—"it's been left to us in his will."

"Holy smoke," said Eddie. "I can't tell anyone?"

"Not until we do first," Lawrence said sternly.

"So you've actually been inside?"

"Not yet."

"Here," Eddie said, "take this then, and see if he cut the pages. I really want to know." Lawrence took the little slip of paper and stuck it in his breast pocket.

A man had come in and was unlocking his box, a farmer from out in the country. Lawrence recognized him but could not recall his name, so he only gave a brief wave. "Will this go out today, Eddie?" The young postmaster took the bright yellow envelope and assured him it would.

On his way back to work, Lawrence contemplated the interior of 17 Phelps Street that Nancy had not been able to discern through the drawn curtains. He doubted it had been dusted or mopped in years. There would be an old man smell to it. There would be knobs missing from doors and bureau drawers that stuck and chains that no longer pulled on lights and dripping faucets, moldy cupboards, a lumpy sagging mattress with unwashed sheets and moth-eaten blankets and a flattened pillow on a creaky bed frame, all the comforts gone that had hardly mattered to an old recluse.

When Lawrence strode into his bank with the dark blue block letters on the glass door, he was beckoned aside by the loan officer. She had taken a call from the lawyer. "He said he could 'get you in on Wednesday the fourteenth at noon, if that suits.' Get you in where, Lawrence?"

He leaned over her desk and said under his breath, "The judge's house, Helen."

"You're buying it?" she whispered. "I'd heard it was a possibility."

For now, Lawrence decided to confide no further. "It's a possibility" was all he would say, hoping Eddie Boyce would keep his talkative mouth shut for a little while.

INSIDE THE HOUSE

That day, the Illinois Senate impeached Governor Blagojevich, and it was all over TV at suppertime. Nancy Huggins was not ready to tell her husband about Will Turley's awful scars, nor did Lawrence Huggins want yet to disclose the extent of the Turley trust fund. Why they felt they must keep their findings secret from each other neither quite knew. It made them mildly uncomfortable, but in an oddly excited sense. Each had come somewhat closer to solving the mystery of their neighbor's strange life.

For Nancy, however, there was a horrifying new element. Once she had gotten past her own great upset, she was filled with greater sorrow than ever for Will himself. She always assumed he had come from a good family, but she also knew that abuse occurred in so-called good families. "Good" was the surface, what the world could see. White families from the wealthier suburbs were all good in that manner, and Will had come from—was it Winnetka or Wilmette? He had mentioned it once. Nancy knew he had no brothers or sisters. It was tricky getting his story out of him. She could not say, "So, Will, tell us about yourself." He would only suck in a wrinkly cheek and exhale "pfff" as if to say, "Nothing worth mentioning," and go back to eating his supper. Not that he was rude. He would make a sly grin or a kindly wink to let them know he would divulge no details. But when Nancy referred to Chloe as an only child, "Like me" had popped out from his lips before his next spoonful of soup. His evident embarrassment kept the Hugginses from probing further. And how had the W-town come up? Lawrence was saying he hoped to manage one of the AmTrust branches on the

North Shore before he retired, and Will said, "You wouldn't like it. I grew up in W—" Nancy decided it was Winnetka, the wealthier of the two. Maybe Lawrence remembered. They had always figured Will came from money if he had lived out here all these years without doing a day's work. But now she knew he also came from a bad home, the bad beneath the good. Surely it was his father who had inflicted those wounds.

Lawrence's new knowledge had led him to other conclusions. Rose Carron said he and Nancy might have been the nicest people in William Turley's life, but he was now surer there had been someone much nicer, and he knew his name: Private Caleb Pitchley of the U.S. Army. It was fitting that he was only a private. And the names were so similar. "Pitchley, Turley, Turley, Pitchley" had been rocking back and forth in Lawrence's brain ever since Rose pointed out the humor in it. It was like a washing machine agitating or the Tilt-A-Whirl he and Nancy had made the mistake of riding at the Sinnissippi County Fair last summer. Lawrence had never known a Caleb. The name sounded biblical. It could even have been a black name in the old days when everyone had names from the Bible. Pitchley could be a black name too. But what black man in the Korean War could have taken out a million dollar life insurance policy? Well, what was a million-plus now was then maybe only a hundred thousand. Lawrence knew that a few of these country white people had nearly a million stashed away. Dr. Artie Pratt surely had that much in assets. In Chicago, black businessmen, higher-ups at the bank like Hirsch or Hub, and lawyers, doctors—they had plenty more. Lawrence confessed to himself how irked he was that the Vermont cousin was coming into that million-three after never having done a kindness to deserve even a penny of it. It somehow made the house seem less of a gift, despite Rose having said it was what truly mattered to the dead man. Will should have left his trust fund to the county that had tolerated him all these many years. He should have endowed the school, the library, the hospital. No one had ever bothered him here or teased or tormented or hurt him. He had found a safe refuge from the intrusions of the world. Had he no gratitude for that? Gratitude only for a dozen or so home-cooked suppers? Some young soldier had died fighting for his country and left the means to keep his friend William Turley in comfort and safety for life and old Will had passed that gift on to an unknown cousin? That was how white folk stayed rich. No black man would have done what he did.

Next Wednesday at the lunch hour, Nancy's Forester was pulling up out front behind a silver Lexus when Lawrence rounded the corner on foot from the bank. On the side porch of number 17 stood a bleached-haired woman in a long black suede coat and boots and black leather gloves. Nancy stepped from the wagon and took her husband's hand to navigate the front walk, though it was freshly sanded by Felipe Reyes.

"I'm Serena Ross from Ryleston Properties," the woman announced, slipping off her right glove to shake their hands. "It's quite the house. You could do some interesting things with it." She jiggled her key in the lock. As the door swung open, the enamel oval with its whippoorwill flashed in a ray of the noon sun. "We're setting it at fifty-five," she said, "so keep your coats on."

The vestibule held only a brass coat rack with Will's black furled umbrella leaning below and his light spring khaki jacket hanging from a hook. He had died in his heavy winter coat, hat, and mittens. Nancy gulped at the thought.

Lawrence had followed Serena into the front hall, where an ornate oaken stairway ascended, no stair carpet, no rug on the floor, but a border inlayed in darker wood.

"Front parlor," said the realtor indicating the arched doorway, the dark woodwork intricately carved, where in their own hall it was plain. Nancy was casting her eyes around what she had barely glimpsed in setting sunlight the few times Will had neglected to draw the curtains.

"And pocket doors to the back parlor." Serena demonstrated by sliding them out and back again.

"By God!" said Lawrence stepping through. "We knew there were books but, Nancy—in here, all these wooden cabinets with glass doors, all these old books!"

"And here in the front parlor," Nancy said, "didn't you notice? Shelves and shelves and shelves on each wall. There's more books than the library has! And only an armchair—and this is like a library table with cubbies below, all filled, too."

"It's an octagon table," said Serena, "a valuable piece. Mr. Turley must've had those front parlor shelves built in because, behind them, see, the faded old flowery wallpaper? Mrs. Gale changed nothing after the judge died, and she lived on here for thirty years. The back parlor would've been Judge Gale's study. I expect the glass-fronted cabinets were for his law books. Oh, but there's open shelves in every other room. Upstairs, they're of cheap pine. Mr. Turley must've hired someone from town, unless he built them himself. He obviously had a mania for books. You'll want to tear out all the shelves, except for in the study. The front parlor could be lovely with the old wallpaper stripped off and some light let in." She swept over to the far wall, the western bay, and yanked back the heavy curtains. "Look! And the front window, too, see! But we'll keep them closed for now. Go investigate the upstairs." She set about drawing the curtains again with her gloved hands.

"What will we ever do with all these books!" Nancy asked her husband.

"There's plenty more upstairs," sang Serena after them. "Mr. Ryleston's wife's an interior designer—Lydia Ryleston, she's done over many old homes. You should consult her. And she might be interested in some of these nicely bound old sets to do people's dens."

Lawrence had climbed the stairs. "There's so little furniture," he said to Nancy behind him. "But where's the reading room where he always sat?"

"To the right," said Nancy.

They both stood in the doorway and looked in. Every wall held books, paperbacks mostly, and there was a rotating fan sitting unplugged in the corner and a deep-cushioned armchair with a hassock, its fuzzy brown upholstery worn down on the arms, and a wooden rocker with a pillow of blue ticking scrunched on the seat. "It hasn't been fluffed up since he sat on it," said Nancy picking up a small volume bound in red leather that lay open there. "He was reading this before he went out on his last errand," she said. "He put on his coat and mittens and his hat with the flaps, remember, and he died and never came home." Tears welled in her eyes as she held the book under the reading lamp that stood between the chairs. She waited for Lawrence to find the knob to switch it on. "*The Private Papers of Henry Ryecroft,*" she read, "by George Gissing. So it's a novel? The book he never finished reading."

"Leave it open where he left it," Lawrence said. "I wonder what was the last sentence he ever read."

"He was at the end of a chapter. This is probably it." Then, Nancy read aloud, " 'The mint is there, and we know it; yet our palate knows only the young potato.' "

"Not very significant for the last sentence of a lifetime," said Lawrence. "We ought to finish his reading for him, but it sounds like a bizarre sort of book."

He had not meant to be critical, and Nancy did not take it as such because now tears were on her cheeks. "I'll leave it just as it was." She placed the book, spine up and open, on the flattened pillow.

"Potato!" said Lawrence. "His last word. But remember him saying how words passed right along and disappeared one after the other to make room for the next?"

"He said it would be a burden to have to remember them all."

"Now I'm afraid I'll remember *potato* forever," said Lawrence, this time trying a smile to cheer Nancy up.

"What do you think?" came the realtor's voice up the stairs. They heard the clicks of her high-heeled boots on the landings and then coming their way. "It's surprisingly clean, isn't it?" she said. "The pantry's full of brooms and mops and rags and dusters. We left everything in the kitchen except perishables. Even the bathroom is spotless. Did you look? He didn't have anyone in to clean, did he? I suppose he had little to do but polish and dust. The windowpanes are the only disaster areas, but he never seemed to want to look out."

"We never saw him in a window, except his silhouette here on the shade," said Lawrence going to try rolling it up, but it had lost its spring and only rose a foot. "Enough to let in a breeze on a hot day," he said. "The only other window facing our house, besides the stained glass in the stairwell, must be his kitchen downstairs, but he kept that shade down, too."

The two large bedrooms over the front and back parlors were empty but for more bookshelves. Only the small bedroom at the back, next to the bath, held no books. There was a neatly made single bed with spindle head and footboards. "Another valuable piece," said Serena Ross from Ryleston Properties.

On the bedside table's lower shelf there was, however, one heavy book, still sealed in the plastic wrap that had protected it for shipping. "One he hadn't gotten around to yet," said Nancy. She switched on the reading lamp and held it to the light. Through the plastic, she read the title: *Finnegans Wake*. "Look, Lawrence, the invoice is dated July 29, 1990. Nineteen years ago! I guess he was saving this one for later."

"Let's leave it where it was," said Lawrence. "If we didn't know Will better, we might've expected a Bible by his bed."

"Not a religious man, I gather," said Serena. "Perhaps the schools or the public library would like some of these books. They should go to a good cause."

Nancy had stuck her head in the bathroom, with its clawfoot tub and pedestal sink and a wooden-seat toilet with the tank up on the wall and a pull chain. It was all as spotless as Serena had said, and the toilet paper roll was just begun. An unnerving thought to have: the last squares of toilet paper he ever used, the last time he did anything he ever had to do, Nancy thought, every mundane thing's final last time.

Lawrence was in a strange state of mind as well. He had been wandering through a blurry landscape of bindings and titles. He had barely looked into the bathroom or noticed they were now descending the back stairs to the kitchen.

"Amazing, isn't it?" the bleached-haired woman's voice was saying. "And we found it just like this—immaculate! We've left the canned goods and unopened jars in the cupboards."

"What an ancient fridge, Lawrence, like Granny Jo's," said Nancy.

"And the dining room—the sideboard's practically empty. I gather Mrs. Gale's children took all they wanted and left what they probably saw as hideous old Victorian pieces. It seems Mr. Turley didn't add a thing."

"More bookshelves in the dining room, Lawrence," said Nancy.

He felt only the floorboards beneath his heavy shoes. The walls had disappeared behind books and books and books. Somehow, he made it to the front parlor again and thought to look for those red books sent from Australia to see if the pages had been cut, but there were so many books, red, blue, green, black. He did not know where to start looking.

Nancy was saying she had to get back to the hospital. Her eyes were dry now, and she was buttoning up her coat and arranging her knit scarf.

"How did he know where each book was?" Lawrence said aloud to himself.

"Come, Lawrence, she has to lock up. It was nice of you, Serena, to let us see what we've taken on."

"I was over here anyway. We're handling some properties in a new addition outside town. Nothing at all there like this lovely old home. So nice to meet you, Dr. Huggins."

"Nancy."

"Nancy."

"I think it's alphabetized by author," Lawrence said.

"And you really could do some interesting things. Here, let me give you Lydia's card. How I'd love to see that front parlor with the shelves ripped out!'"

"It goes all the way to Z," said Lawrence kneeling down to pull out the last volume on the bottom shelf by the archway: *Truth*, by Emile Zola. Thumbing through it, Lawrence thought it an ironic title for a novel since novels were fictitious.

"My husband could explore here all day."

"What surprises me," he said to the two women, "is that all these books seem to be novels. I expected old Will to read history and philosophy and biographies of famous people, and books on nature and geography—"

"That's just one room," Nancy said. "Maybe he's got it all arranged like a library. Susie Gitchell would love it here. She's our town librarian," she told Serena. "Come on, Lawrence, it's awful chilly."

"He never could have read all these books," he said. His knees gave a creak when he stood up.

Then, the realtor flicked off the ceiling light in the hall, and from the dimness the three of them stepped out into the brilliance of the sun shining up off the snow.

THEIR SECRETS

ack at his desk, Lawrence could not concentrate. All of 2008 was wrapped up and done with; all accounts had begun anew. Everyone's income, earned and unearned, was being tabulated now. Taxes had all been withheld, paid quarterly, or were yet to be paid, all deductions were being figured, all rents and royalties and tips and wages, over the counter if not under, all interest and dividends—all was being totted up, ready for Internal Revenue to commence closing the books on another year, a shaky year, 2008, but a year ending in a hopeful prospect that things might yet be turned around, saved, set on a more judicious track, equitable, honest, secure. And all Lawrence Huggins could think of now was William Turley's library. The house itself had faded away, leaving bookshelves upon bookshelves suspended in the cold stuffy air. He had all that insurance money, and all he did with it was fill rooms and rooms with books!

Lawrence made some calculations. Each shelf was, say, a yard long. Say a book averaged an inch and a half thick. The old ones might be two inches, but there were newer, thinner ones and lots of paperbacks, so say an inch and a half. That meant twenty-four or, to make it easier, twenty-five per shelf. There were eight shelves in each rank, so that's two hundred books. The main rooms, two up and two down, were the same dimensions as at 19 Phelps Street, sixteen by twenty. Leave off half for windows and doors and odd corners, so that's thirty-six feet in twelve ranks of two hundred. Twenty-four hundred books per room. Plus the dining room and upstairs study, maybe half that in each, so twenty-four hundred times five makes twelve thousand books. It's impossible to read that much in a lifetime. Even cut out a couple thousand. *Truth*, whose pages he had flipped through, was very fat and had large print. So say ten thousand books of varying lengths. And Will was seventy-six years old. He came here at twenty-one. But he had probably been reading all his life. Make him sixteen when he was old enough to read the sorts of books his house was filled with. So sixty years of reading—sixty goes into twelve thousand two hundred times, but not as neatly into ten thousand: one hundred and sixty-six and two-thirds of a book. Somewhere between that and two hundred, given three hundred and sixty-five days a year, comes out to about one book every two days. And all out loud? By reading eight or ten hours a day, Lawrence conceded, it might even be doable.

But surely, Will had begun slower at sixteen, and perhaps in later years he had slowed down again. And why assume he had read every single book anyway? There was the one he had been saving wrapped in plastic by his bed. There might be many more such. And maybe there were duplicates. How to know which ones he had read? They would not all have needed their pages cut, only the oldest ones. Maybe Will had not tried to read three or four books a week. Eddie Boyce would have said so if packages came into the post office at quite that rate. But there had been the heavy cartons Mrs. Gitchell remembered, probably those big old books in multi-volume sets. They could have kept Will busy for months. How did he even remember which ones he had read? And how did his voice hold out? From what they occasionally heard on summer nights, Will did not always read quietly to himself but gave passionate full voice to certain pages, and when characters were talking, his voice went up and down, louder and softer, a kind of speaking music behind the window shade of his reading room, the only music at 17 Phelps— no radio, no TV, no record player. The only electrically powered things he had were lamps and the fan and the fridge and the Hoover out in the pantry. And no telephone—there must be no intrusion from outside. Now the old man's silent self-absorbed world sank down upon Lawrence's thoughts as he sat at his desk with the chatter of tellers and patrons out front and his desktop's wallpaper displaying his girl Chloe, hard at work at her own desk up in Wisconsin with an open book before her and a stack of more books to one side. Deet had snapped the photo, and she had emailed it with the caption: "Workin' hard, Dads!"

Lawrence peered at the titles in the stack: *Home and Exile, Hopes and Impediments, No Longer at Ease*—sad titles, he thought. They were all by one of her favorite authors, Chinua Achebe. He had tried to read one called *Things Fall Apart* but found it hard going, though he told Chloe he liked it. He believed Chinua Achebe was still alive, so Will Turley's library would not include those books if it included any by black authors at all. What will their scholarly daughter make of Will's vast library?

*****

Meanwhile, Dr. Nancy Huggins had a boy's bleeding lip to stitch up. Blubbering little Jaxson Moultree was only five. He had fallen, running up the icy steps to his front door, and cut himself—"Badly," said his fat mom, but Nancy knew it was only the blood. It required a single quick stitch while the boy sniffled and whimpered, determined to be brave enough not to scream. His mom was squeezing his trembling hand tightly, and all the while Nancy said happy things about him going home and making a snowman, and what could he use for the nose, and maybe he could give the snowman a tiny twig stitch on his lip to show how brave they both were. Mrs. Moultree's eyes were blinking furiously to hold in her tears. She could not bring herself to watch.

"All done, Jax!" Nancy said while deftly placing her implements out of sight. "It always looks worse than it is. Blood's a healthy thing, Jax. It cleaned out your lip so it won't get infected."

He was gazing at her out of foggy blue eyes, trying to pay attention.

"And that's a really cool stitch you've got. It'll fall right off without hurting after it's done its job. Just don't tug at it, promise?"

"It's tough-looking," said his mom.

"See, Jax," Nancy said holding up a mirror as she carefully wiped off the last red smears.

"Wow," said the bucktoothed little boy.

"Say thank you to Dr. Nancy," his mom prompted.

"He may not feel too thankful at the moment," Nancy said, "but I do have something for him." She reached into a cabinet for one of the plastic VW Bugs she kept for boys who had had reason to be scared.

"Wow," said Jax.

"It's only for the brave boys."

Mrs. Moultree took Nancy's hand in her clammy pink one and whispered, "Oh thanks, oh gosh, I thought I was going to die driving him over. He was screaming blue murder."

"No, I wasn't!" said Jaxson heading for the door with his car.

When they had gone, Nancy washed up then checked her computer to find she had fifteen minutes before Shayla Lundt's appointment. She could go to her office, but the consulting room seemed peacefuller. No one would come in, no one would call, she would not look at the screen again, she would sit and breathe deeply. Rushing back from Phelps Street, she had had no chance to think while eating the cold sandwich she had left on her front seat. Now she was hungry again and tired, and it was only 3:30.

Those spotless empty rooms of Will's were haunting her. He had lived in such sparkling clean emptiness. The worn old floorboards were waxed and shiny and smooth. Nancy had run her finger along a bookshelf and found not a mote of dust. Where would dust even come from in that tightly sealed house? Will opened his front door only a few times a week and the kitchen door only to take out the trash. The fireplaces in the parlors held no specks of ash. There were no rugs to host mites, only two armchairs, one up and one down, and the tightly made bed. But for the one open book about potatoes on the pillow of the rocking chair, it seemed no one had ever lived there. If that book had been on its proper shelf, there would not even have been that much evidence, only the flattened pillow where a heavy body had recently rested, had sat there for years, for decades. The pillow was well past puffing back up on its own.

Nancy could not dispel the thought of their dead neighbor inhabiting such a grand empty library for so many years. She tried to imagine him moving in at age twenty-one. The Gale family had cleared out everything they cared to keep. He would have to make do with what was left for him, and it was sufficient. He had no thought of anything as a "valuable piece" but needed only a bed, a table, a chair, some old crockery and flatware, the old appliances. However little money he may have had, surely he could have bought a soft rug, a comfortable sofa to curl up on. But all the needs of the young man, with scars still fresh on his tender skin, were shelves filled with books. They were to be his comfort, and Nancy had some notion of how that could be. But his sole comfort?

The judge's study, emptied of law books, must have inspired young Will. Likely, he had brought some books of his own to start filling up those shelves. He must have been collecting books before he arrived here. He must have escaped into books all his young life. And when he had used up the judge's shelves, he would have built more, built them himself or hired a carpenter. Nancy would ask Susie Gitchell, who had grown up across the street. She must have seen the lumber delivered, heard the hammering and sawing. As a girl, Susie saw him as a romantic hero come to her backwater town, aloof and mysterious to a girl who would spend her life working in a library. I will tell her first, Nancy decided, she deserves to know what we have done. We will invite her in as soon as we get the key. She will know what to make of all those books. We can donate them to the Rockvale Public Library, make it the best small town library in Illinois. Nancy wondered if she was turning town-proud. Chloe had warned them against getting too stuck in their sleepy rural life. "It's a danger for old folks," she told them. Old folks! We were born about the time Will Turley moved out here, Nancy realized. That was a measure of how long he had lived alone in that house and spoken so few words to so few people on his rare ventures into town.

Nancy thought back to her psychiatry rotation. His behavior was surely not a mere eccentricity, it was evidence of a severe disorder, if not a psychosis, benign to the world but not to Will himself. Then she thought again of his scars. The cleanliness and orderliness of the house. Perhaps Will Turley had suffered a childhood, an adolescence, so disordered and unclean, so beyond his control, so malignant and brutal, that he had to create for himself a perfect refuge, a library of the past, all categorized and alphabetized and safely shelved and dusted and then, slowly over the years, all read aloud in his own voice echoing in the silent rooms, all that had once been written down, now made his own.

Then why had he dared come eat supper with his new neighbors and said such thoughtful things? And the vexing question Nancy had asked herself many times but now could ask again, having learned so much more: why leave us his house and all his treasure? Her shoulders gave a shudder, and she had to shake out her arms to start up her circulation again. She feared her body had come to a complete stop.

Presently, she must attend to Shayla Lundt, who was entering puberty at age eleven and wanted, her mother reported, to talk about it privately with her doctor, so she was coming unattended.

*****

At supper, when they could finally relax, the Hugginses each knew it was time to tell the secret things they had been keeping to themselves. Lawrence shut off the TV with its reports on the governor's upcoming trial and the preparations underway for next week's inauguration. "I've come to a new feeling about Will Turley," he said when he had sat down, pulled his napkin from its ring, and spread it on his lap. He ladled the chili into their bowls while Nancy tossed the salad.

"Poor Will," she said.

"He was not exactly poor, honey. Pass the cornbread?"

"I didn't mean it that way. I know he had money or how could he have lived like that for so long?"

"It's a lot of money, a lot," Lawrence said. "I talked to Rose Carron at her branch. They hold his trust. It's worth well over a million, and it's all going to a hippie cousin he never even met."

"A million!" Nancy put her spoonful of chili back in her bowl.

"A million-three, Rose said. I confess. Remember when I drove your car over there on bank business? Well, I didn't want you thinking I was looking a gift horse in the mouth, but I was, and I shouldn't have, because now I'm angry at our old friend Will. He could have left that money to the county. There could be the new William Turley Wing on your hospital."

"He didn't want people knowing him," said Nancy.

"That's just damn selfish then."

"I'm not defending him, Lawrence. I haven't thought this through yet."

"And it wasn't family money to begin with!"

"But how do we know?"

"Honey, I'm not arguing. I'm telling you something. The money came from a soldier who got killed in the Korean War, his life insurance policy. Rose told me so." With a glum frown, Lawrence began spooning up his chili between bites of cornbread. He took a swig of his beer before looking across at his wife again.

"You're truly upset," she said.

"It's not that I'm envious. I don't even want that damn house with all those crazy books. But I'd have expected more charity from Will."

"You think he should've left it to the county?"

"He could've left it to the Society for the Prevention of Cruelty to Animals! I don't care. But to do some good."

"We just don't know," Nancy said. "Some soldier's insurance? A friend?" She took a forkful of salad wondering how to tell him what she herself had been keeping secret. She did not want to tell him. It was too intimate and shameful even to have learned it. And Artie had told her in confidence, as a fellow physician. "Lawrence?"

"We shouldn't argue, honey. We should be deciding what to do next. We've already accepted the house and all its contents, 'free and clear as is,' to quote Mr. Rod Strite."

"Artie Pratt told me something else about Will," Nancy said.

"Artie? What?"

"I should've told you last week. It got me so distraught. Lawrence, we have to tell each other everything. We've always done so. Why didn't we this time?"

"Tell me what, Nancy, what?"

"Artie told me, in strict confidence, that when he cleaned the body—well, that Will had terrible scars across his back and chest like old wounds, healed but severely scarred over. Will wouldn't take off his clothes when he went in for a checkup. But when Artie had to prepare the body—"

"Honey," Lawrence said reaching across to grasp her hand.

"It was terrible to hear—"

"Oh, poor honey, we've got ourselves into some sorry mess. And poor Will! Old wounds? Nothing that happened out here?"

"Artie said they must have been inflicted in his youth. Maybe he could tell from the way they stretched out as Will grew. Scar tissue doesn't renew the way skin does."

"I don't like thinking about it," said Lawrence.

"It's why I couldn't tell you."

They both tried to eat their supper awhile and ponder. Lawrence downed his beer. Nancy was holding back tears and dabbed at her eyes with her napkin.

Finally Lawrence said, "We have inherited his house." Nancy nodded. "And I thought he'd been living a privileged life, endowed by some pal's insurance policy and studying his books like a monk in a monastery under a vow of silence. But, so, he'd been scourged?"

"That's a church word," Nancy said.

Lawrence set his large hands on either side of his placemat and made a decision. "We must give the books away to a worthy cause. We'll start with that. We don't want them ourselves. And we can put the house and the antiques up for sale and take no profit. Or we can donate it all for some senior center or youth club for the town."

"We have to think this through, Lawrence. Let's not make any plans yet. It's so new. We don't know how we'll truly feel in our own good time."

THEIR QUESTIONS

On Monday, all AmTrust branches had been closed for King Day but were not for Tuesday's inauguration. Just as well. Lawrence had worried that someone might come in to cash a check and, finding the bank closed, think the manager was favoring the man of his own race who was being sworn in. But he did give himself a long lunch hour to go home and watch.

Nancy could not get off work but caught glimpses of the ceremony on the waiting room TV between patients while her husband sat alone at home with a cup of coffee and two hot slices from the Greek's. It was a cold day in D.C., but there they stood, thousands of Americans, bringing water to the eyes of a black bank manager in northwestern Illinois, where he had never imagined he would live, anymore than he had imagined a half-African man swearing the oath of George Washington.

Lawrence had read that the outgoing vice president, who was attending in a wheelchair, was something like a thirteenth cousin to the new president through his white side. The Huggins lineage could be traced to the same Old World continents. British blood was mixed with his African blood, the blood of the American South, of Leesville, Louisiana, where his great-great-grandfather came up from. The other side, the Lawrences, were from Mississippi, Yazoo City, and the Sublettes were from Washington, Georgia, where Grandfather Sublette himself was born in the 1890s. And on Nancy's mother's side it was Barbuda in the Caribbean, which people confused with Barbados and Bermuda and old Granny Jo had to explain it had been a slave colony, an island none of her people would ever care to return to. She had stories from her own grandparents and had passed them down.

But before that, where had they come from, from what land? The new president was half Kenyan, he knew his people and what language they spoke as well as he knew his British parentage. But the countries of West Africa were Europe's inventions. The Portuguese took this one, the British that, the French another—Ivory Coast, Gold Coast, Slave Coast, that was all they were. The Hugginses were more likely to be cousin to President Obama through his British blood than his African. Kenya was too far from where Lawrence's ancestors had been led away in chains. It was a French slaver, Lawrence decided, if they had been brought to Louisiana. He had studied the map to learn the names of towns—Dakar, Conakry, Kankan, Bamako—but he could never know for certain. Yet the Huggins name must have come from an Englishman or Scot who had forced the brutal mixing.

Cousin Gertrude was the family historian. She had never married but had made it her job to counsel the troubled and take in the strays. She had been a big sister to Lawrence, who himself had no sister or brother, and she had been a mother to him when his own mother died. She had tended his father on his deathbed, and now she had let their Chloe bring her sophisticated theatrical Deet into her home. Gertrude Huggins was the person Lawrence measured himself against, lived up to, strove for—his father's older brother's daughter, the woman left warming the family hearth. And now, he told himself, it was she who deserved to inherit a solid brick house, but Trudy would only pass it on to her younger cousins. And therefore, so should he, Lawrence resolved as he watched the screen and listened and wiped at his eyes. He wished for Nancy to be there beside him.

But she had missed the oath while treating a child for strep. Only later could she stand in the waiting room long enough to catch most of the address. She had a sense that the few old people seated there were keeping their mouths shut after she joined them. What might they have been saying to each other if she were not there? One old lady glanced over at her now and then, perhaps to detect a trace of the racial pride, even of triumph, that indeed Nancy was feeling. Of course, she was feeling it! How could she not feel it, and why shouldn't she? She allowed her smile to broaden then caught the lady simply nodding back up at her. Maybe they were sharing a happiness. Let me assume, Nancy told herself, that all of us in this room feel happy that such a moment has come to our nation. I will go on assuming so, until I hear otherwise. An old white gentleman in overalls, a farmer from out of town, exclaimed, "He's right!" Nancy saw his wife beside him touch his hand. Then Dr. Huggins was paged back to her office.

As the afternoon passed by, her ponderings of the previous week found the stray free moment to skitter about in Nancy's brain. Nothing had been settled. In church on Sunday, she had, with a full heart, joined in the prayer for the new president and the country and for a just resolution to the troubles of the state of Illinois and had wondered if she and Lawrence might consult Pastor Miller on their dilemma. Perhaps the Methodist Church could make use of the Turley house—the judge's house—as after fifty years it was still known. Or Pastor Miller might counsel the proper manner in which to dispose of the gift and still honor the giver, for Will had surely intended something in passing to his neighbors all that had enriched his solitary life. Nancy had come to see the house itself as merely a repository for the gift, which was his collection of books. He had purposefully left it to them, rather than to the public library or the high school or the college over in the next county and thereby had burdened them with a responsibility they had no desire to bear. Lawrence was angry at him for it, and maybe Nancy was too, but she could not quite feel it as anger. What was it? Was she taking too seriously this capricious notion of a delusional old man who had fixated on the Hugginses as his spiritual heirs? They would surely never read his books. They could never treasure them as he did.

Then, in her next minute between patients, it came to Nancy that in utter sanity William Turley had chosen them as the good people who would know best how to preserve that treasure. He had sent them on a quest he could not undertake, shy and wounded as he was. In his utter isolation, he could not ensure a haven for his books without appointing a shepherd, two shepherds, to watch over them. Had he bequeathed his library to an institution, whoever then could guarantee it would not be auctioned off in lots, divided, the rare items—if there were any—sold to dealers, the common stuff plundered at rummage sales or finally dumped out with the trash? Will Turley saw his books as a completeness never to be separated, not child from parent, brother from sister, husband from wife, never to be unalphabetized, disorganized, scattered. All right, Nancy told herself, yes, his was one sort of madness, but she understood Will now as he had meant to be understood, and she would explain it to Lawrence and hope he also would understand.

Or was she simply discombobulated by her sixty seconds here and there on this busy afternoon, her thoughts disjointed as in a dream that would make little sense when she got home for supper?

Lawrence was hardly thinking of Will's books at all when he sat back down at his desk for the last hours of the work day. He had been lifted up by what he had witnessed on his big TV screen at home and had been cheerily greeted by Millie Stover, back from her own lunch hour. She, too, had watched the inauguration and bubbled with excitement, praising the man, loving America, and seeming strangely proud to have Lawrence as her boss. Her sweet expression, eyes and lips and the way she kept clasping her hands, had filled him with joy. So when at his desk the image of the brick house he was soon to own rose once more in his mind's eye, he could only see it as something for the good. He would call Cousin Trudy right now, to talk about the inauguration, of course, but also to seek her guidance about the property. The Gertrude Huggins Home, he felt like calling it, a refuge for wayward children, for the homeless and destitute of Sinnissippi County, regardless of race. *What dreams am I dreaming?* he asked himself with a snort. So, for a dose of reality, he quickly punched in Trudy's number, but no one answered. She must be out with her lady friends celebrating this remarkable day.

And when wife and husband sat down at their supper table and had talked it all over—the oath of office that Nancy had missed and the president's address and the faces in the crowd—and were now looking forward to the evening's coverage of the inaugural balls and the clips recapping the day and the pundits' analyses—when they had finally paused over cups of coffee, Nancy asked, "What do you suppose Will Turley wanted us to do with his books?"

"You're still thinking of that? Let's not bother about it today of all days."

"But I can't help asking myself what he expected of us," Nancy said.

"We'll wait until tomorrow, honey," said Lawrence, though he had also been mulling over their inheritance.

HIS WISHES

Two nights later, a time did come to try recalling things Will had told them and to search for hints. They sat on the sofa in the living room with the other house lurking behind them across the snowy yard.

"So," Nancy began, "you still want to give it all away?"

"We'd be the same as we were," said Lawrence, "and we could do some good. We might start by putting a little money into the house to make it more presentable."

"But we can't afford to if we ever expect to move back and buy in Chicago. We have to be realistic, honey. There's still taxes, and if we put money into it—"

"I know, I know."

"On the other hand, we don't know what capital gains are on selling inherited second homes."

"We'd work it all out, Nancy. If we donate it and write off the improvements, it's all charitable—"

"But what's charitable? Would it be charitable to dispose of Will's property?"

"He couldn't have expected us to live in two houses at once. He was giving us the property, honey. Property! We could switch houses if you think that's what he wanted and then donate ours. But why should we disrupt our comfortable temporary life here to follow the wishes of a dead man we barely knew?"

"It's all so strange," said Nancy slipping her hand into her husband's so as not to feel any rift between them. "Before Artie Pratt told me about the scars, I thought I understood it better."

"And before we saw the house and all those books!" said Lawrence. "No matter what, we'll have to get rid of the books."

"You're still upset about the money going to the cousin."

Lawrence cast a fierce look at her. "How can you say that? You think I only want to give away what we got because we didn't get it all?"

Nancy was squeezing his hand and saying, "No, no, honey."

"You think otherwise I'd want us to live forever in the judge's house next door?"

"No, but we have to get past this distrust between us before we can decide what we're going to do."

"Well, what then?" Lawrence was staring sternly across the room at the blank TV screen.

"Because we have a conflict between—"

He waited for her to explain. She knew that exasperated look, rare as it was.

"—between what's right for us and what Will Turley wanted us to do, and we're not sure what either is."

"I'm sure," said Lawrence. "Not what Will wanted—that doesn't matter—but what's right for us, and that is to come out of this the way we were before he got us into it." He thought a moment then added, "And without losing capital gains tax or creating ill will in Rockvale or problems between the two of us, most of all. And to be able to move back financially comfortable when I'm transferred home. And to leave behind something good for the folks here because they've been good to us and we want to be well remembered."

"That's what Will would've wanted for us?"

"Of course, he would've! He wouldn't want us burdened—or resented, would he?"

"No," Nancy said, "but what did he want for his books?"

"I don't care about his damn books! They're the least of it."

"I don't think so," said Nancy. "I've come to think they're what it's about. That house with its carved moldings and the valuable pieces she kept pointing out wasn't what gave him happiness."

"He sure kept it clean," Lawrence said and tried to laugh.

"But to me it felt more like a house for the books," said Nancy, "and the books are really what he left for us—to keep them together, his collection, as if it was a thing of its own."

"I've said we'll donate them to the library or the high school."

"Remember, Lawrence, how he once said something about happy book-reading childhoods?"

"He meant in general," Lawrence said looking fierce again. He hated when they argued. They seldom did, but this inheritance had brought into their quiet life a disruption he wanted to resolve for good and all, this very night. He no longer had the fondness for Will Turley that Nancy seemed to have, nor any pity for his wounds.

"Happy book-reading childhoods," she said again, "and I did assume he meant his own. But after what Artie told me—well, then I wondered if he had indeed had a happy book-reading childhood he was trying to get back to, before the—"

"Those aren't exactly children's books over there, honey."

"But by sitting there reading he was taken back, I think, sitting in a chair the way he did as a boy reading to himself and feeling safe in made-up worlds. It's the way children read. I've studied this, honey. It's their own imaginary world they make out of the written word. Children don't doubt words in a book. They take them for real. I bet that's how Will still took them. Remember when he said he lived in many other people's lives? Ever since he moved here his whole life was reading. He was having a happy book-reading adulthood with grown-up books. I don't think he regressed like a beaten child. Will didn't have that shiftiness or timidity or that bottled-up rage of beaten small children. What happened to him must've come later, in adolescence, after he'd developed a surer sense of self. He had such a calm way, Lawrence, not depressed or withdrawn, despite living all alone. He was our supper guest, and he said only as much as he chose to. It was frustrating, those old gray eyes peering out of his wrinkly eyelids. Such sharp eyes—he didn't seem to need glasses at all—and somehow I couldn't do the cheerful questioning thing I do with my little patients and their parents because the old man was enjoying himself just as he was. We had to let him be. I suppose we could've said, 'You must've had a happy childhood with all the reading you did, Will, from the way you've been reading ever since.' We could've tried that. Why didn't we? Now I wish we had."

Nancy had talked herself out, so she leaned back against Lawrence's arm draped across the cushion behind her. They were doing better now. He was not arguing back.

He had also been thinking it all through. "I love you, honey," he said.

"Why do you say that?" she asked with a suspicious smirk.

"Because you try to figure people out. You don't go and snap the way I do. You're the good doctor."

"You're good, too. You're the unselfish one who wants to give it all away and help people."

"I'm selfish about us. I want to provide for you and Chloe, and I was thinking of Cousin Trudy and all of them back home and what we could do if that house was only in Chicago, but it's out here where we don't even belong or care for people in that way, and there it is—" He turned his head to the blackness of the windowpane and saw his own face reflected and Nancy's soft head nestled on his shoulder. "We could still get out of it," he whispered to soothe her. "It isn't out of probate. We could change our minds. I could call Rod Strite tomorrow morning first thing."

"No," Nancy murmured, "no, because this has come to us, and we have to find out why."

"You're thinking there's some spiritual reason?"

"Not really spiritual, but—"

"We could speak to Pastor Miller, Nancy."

"About the church using the house?"

"Well, or about why it's come to us, what it means in a Christian sense."

"Will was surely no Christian," Nancy said a bit gruffly.

"But we are," said Lawrence. "Despite what you say, you're taking the gift as something spiritual, I can tell."

"Oh, I don't know how I'm taking it."

"Because you don't want to get rid of those books," he said.

"It's that I don't want to go picking through them," said Nancy sitting up straight. "I want them to stay together. That's the one thing I'm sure of."

"That sounds crazy, but I suppose it's a place for us to start. Maybe I disagree, but I'll give in to you on that."

"I want you to understand why, Lawrence," she said and lay her head back down on his shoulder and nudged up into his shirt collar.

"It's to honor the dead man's wish," he said. "But he didn't indicate it in the will."

"Going through the house, it's still what I sensed, though."

Lawrence pressed his cheek into her sweet-smelling hair and thought awhile. He remembered how he had felt when the walls of those rooms had gone blurry and he was walking past books and books and books on shelves and shelves and shelves and they were all he saw. So he said, "We could print up nice labels to glue inside each book that say 'The William Turley Collection' and donate it all to the library so they'd have to preserve them in his honor."

"Thousands of labels, honey, and weeks to glue them all in?"

"Cold winter Sunday afternoons with nothing else to do!"

"Chloe would think we'd gone nuts."

"All right, no labels," Lawrence said. "We'll talk to Mrs. Gitchell. The lawyer, the pastor, the librarian—we're not alone, honey. We can even ask Chloe for advice."

"No," said Nancy, "she doesn't have to know about books or antiques or dead men's wishes. For now, let's leave it as our simple new rental property. She can understand that."

"So we're waiting on further decisions?"

"We're not changing our minds, Lawrence. You're not calling Rod Strite. We've taken it on. I'll talk to Susie Gitchell, and we'll both talk to the pastor after church."

"Dr. Huggins has it diagnosed," Lawrence said.

A Letter and the Key

At the bank mid-morning on Friday the loan officer, Helen Van Inwegen, came into Lawrence's office and gently shut the door behind her saying, "If I may?" He looked up and nodded. "Two things," she said. "First, a letter came special delivery from Stark, Weber, Brennheim, and Braun. Here's that. Then this, a fax saying the plumbing contractor from Ryleston Properties will drop off the house key here. It says, given the cousin's letter, they see no reason you shouldn't have access immediately. Here's the fax. I hope you don't mind, I couldn't help reading it."

"That's fine, Helen. It's all still in process."

"So you've really bought the house! The cousin is his heir?"

"It's a bit more complicated, but that's essentially it."

"You're sure it's a wise move?" Helen asked. "We know what the rental market's doing, Lawrence. I don't mean to meddle."

"Probably not the wisest of moves," he said with an unapologetic grin, "and we don't quite yet know what we'll do with it, but hey—"

"Then I hope it means you and Nancy will be settling down here with us. I can't tell you what a difference you've made. We'd all been dreading the merger, but look how well it's turned out. They could've sent me a boss who'd sweep us all out, the way they did with the Riparian bank."

"Our Sinnissippi's still a solid small county bank, Helen. Don't worry. I'm here to keep it that way. We just have more AmTrust clout now. Which reminds me, what's happening with the new signage?"

"I'll check on it," she said and left him with an open door again.

Lawrence unsealed the envelope with some trepidation and unfolded first a sheet from a yellow legal pad on which Rod Strite had scribbled: "Lawrence and Nancy—see enclosed Xerox FYI. Some weird stuff but reassuring about no contest. Be in touch. Rod." He next unfolded a two-page letter typed single-spaced on a manual typewriter in need of a fresh ribbon. The small Os and As were faint, and the machine skipped spaces now and then, but this is what he read:

Jan 19, 2009
Dear Mr. Strite:

Thank you for expediting our amazing windfall. Sue and I are still reeling. Thought I'd let you know some personal info since to you I'm just a name on a document and usually you must get to meet the people you hand over money to. Up here in the mountains we don't have much to do with lawyers, and I sure don't get back to Illinois since my parents died, and anyway I had quite the falling out with my dad back in the 80s over politics and capitalism and racism and sexism and you name it. Basically we stopped talking to each other and I came out here and met Sue, and we've been living the simple life in this little town of two hundred people, give or take, and we're pretty much off the grid except for being stuck buying gas for the truck. I never knew my dad's cousin William Turley, but he must have been sort of like me because he went off to be a hermit before I was born. My dad would never talk about him. My grandmother was a Turley and she was his dad's older sister who married a Lee. Anyway, I gather my dad and his cousin hated each other, or at least my dad hated him and wouldn't talk about him expect to say he was a disgrace. That was my dad's big deal. Some people just were a disgrace. I guess I grew up to be one myself. Now I don't know if cousin William was a "socialist-humanist-pacifist-environmentalist" like me and Sue, except maybe he was a pacifist. He definitely had nothing more to do with an old crackpot like my dad. Dad said cousin William had turned his back on the real world because he couldn't cut it. He despised William. I do have a few memories of my Great

Aunt Madgie and my Great Uncle Tom Turley. They lived down the street when I was growing up on Ridge Avenue. They never talked about their absent son. My great aunt sat in her living room chair reading by the window all day long, that's how I remember her. And her smoking cigarettes of course, and my great uncle, I don't recall much. But he died first then she died. I was maybe six or seven. He was some sort of retired business guy but not a heavy Republican like all the Lees. I think he was anti-war while Dad was a true hawk, but by the time I got wise to things, the Vietnam War was history and then when Reagan got in, that's when the fur began to fly between me and my dad. I never knew his cousin William had this kind of money! If my dad knew about it he must have been ripped. I don't know a thing about this Caleb Pitchley person and his insurance policy or why that would have been. My dad never mentioned anything like that, and Dad's been dead five years and my mom three, so even if I wanted to ask them I couldn't. My poor mom suffered under Dad but would never say a word against him. We wrote each other and I'd come back and see them when they got old and especially when he got colon cancer. We finally had a passable relationship if we stayed away from anything that mattered. My Sue was sweet with them. And we did get some dough after Mom died. But they never talked about William Turley who had been as good as dead to my dad since the early 50s, I'd guess. I certainly never heard how his hermit cousin supported himself out there. Thinking it over now, Sue and I've been speculating. Maybe there was something gay between this Caleb Pitchley and him and that's why Pitchley left him his insurance policy and that's why William had to leave home, but I can't quite picture Great Uncle Tom as a homophobe though in those days, we're talking fifty-plus years ago, everybody probably was. But all I knew as a kid was my great uncle and aunt had a son who never got married and lived off in the country and maybe wrote them or something but he never came home and they never went to see him as far as I knew. And my sister Abby, who I'm still in regular touch with despite her being married to a super-rich Chicago banker, doesn't remember any more than I do. We certainly never heard of this Pitchley thing until your bank people told us about it. Abby thinks it's oxymoronic that I'm a millionaire now. Of course it's drops in the bucket to her and Carl. She says she'd like to see how much of a commie I am now, having my stocks and bonds and dividends and proxies like a true American. Well, Abigail, we'll just see, won't we! And as for William Turley's neighbors who got the house, tell them I'm sure they're decent people to have meant so much to the old cousin I never met who left me all his dough to do with as I see fit. I suspect it was his dying wish to take a final swipe at my dad, John Lee, Jr., for throwing me out of the house in 1983 and for the way he called Will a disgrace all those years. You must deal with a lot of twisted family psychodrama in your line of work. I hope I haven't offended you with this rant of mine but sometimes it's important to get it out there, the truth behind family money. Sue thinks I go bonkers sometimes but she puts up with me and we have a pretty damn sweet life and three smarty-pants kids we're going to put through college, thanks to William Turley, because this measly country doesn't believe in free higher education, let alone health care for all or gun control or conservation, don't get me started! I've got our kids to think of, don't I? OK, Sue, I'll stop now but you can't read it because I'm putting it in an envelope and sealing it up as soon as I sign it, which I will shortly do with many thanks to you, Mr. Rod Strite.

Sincerely,
John Lee III

No sooner had Lawrence folded up the letter and tucked it back in the envelope than Helen Van Inwegen ahemed at his door and handed him a small cardboard box saying, "The plumber just dropped this off. It's your key."

*****

Dr. Nancy Huggins was driving home from the hospital exhausted and bored after a day of uncooperative whiny little brats and their irresponsible fat mothers. She did not in truth feel that way, but she indulged in a short bout of self-pity because it often helped, and by the time she had come in the back door and pulled off her boots she had left the day behind and was happy to be in her own kitchen with the smell of a chicken roasting and the prospect of a quieting glass of Chablis. Lawrence had set the table in the dining room, for a change, and even lit the candles and put two wine glasses on the sideboard beside the bottle he must have just removed from the fridge and uncorked. She heard his heavy footsteps coming down the stairs.

"Thank you, honey," she said. "I needed to come home to this."

"You said you'd be late, so it's almost ready. I got home early. It's been a most interesting day." He poured out their glasses and followed her to the table.

"What's this?" Nancy saw a brass key lying on her plate. Lawrence was beaming at her. She picked up the key and held it to the shining candle flame. "To next door?" He nodded. "Already?"

"Sit down now, and read this letter." He handed her the folded typewritten sheets.

"You're being mysterious. An old letter of Will's?"

"Look at the date. Strite sent us the Xerox copy."

"My word!" said Nancy as soon as she checked for the signature.

"You read it; I'll put supper on." He left her in candlelight and went back to the kitchen.

When she finally lay the pages down and looked up to find her plate full and her wine yet untasted, Lawrence was raising his glass from across the table, so she clinked hers to it, took a sip, and then searched his wide-eyed stare. "Honey" was all she could think to say.

"Honey back at you!"

Then she said, "He's sure some kind of character, this John Lee the Third. It's something how these white suburban kids end up millionaires, no matter their lefty politics."

"Though this one seems a rather odd case," said Lawrence.

"Well, I'm with his sister Abby. I hope she rubs it in good. I wonder if you'd know her super-rich banker husband."

"Honey, is it you now who's a bit envious?"

"I'm certainly not."

"Good, me neither. Now." He gave her a decisive nod. "But what about this John Lee's idea that Will was paying back his dad for—"

"You think it's his dad who hurt Will?" Nancy asked

"He threw his own son out of the house, didn't he? He's as likely to have tortured his cousin for disgracing the family with something unseemly concerning this Caleb Pitchley person. But I don't see Will Turley as having been, as he puts it, gay. I don't see him as ever having any sexual desires at all. There was no one in his life, no one for fifty years and more, no dirty rumors around town, no other soul ever even set foot in that house." He could see Nancy puzzling over this. "Eat your supper," he said.

So they both dug in and pondered the letter until Nancy said, "I guess it likely was the cousin, John Lee's father. I suppose he has to be the one who hurt Will, whatever the reason."

"At least our young Mr. Strite's learning something of human nature," Lawrence said. "Estate law's giving him an education." Then after a bite of chicken and a follow-up scoop of green peas, Lawrence added, "It might have been wishful thinking about no contest from the Vermont cousin, but the letter clears that up. It's all ours now."

He raised his glass to Nancy again, but she did not quite feel like raising hers.

At the Library

In the morning Nancy made Lawrence promise not to take the key and go snooping until she had seen Susie Gitchell at the library. On cold Saturday mornings that was where a number of mothers dumped their sons and daughters with the volunteer storyteller, Judy Stover, Elsie's sister-in-law, while they drove to the mall in Riparian County for the week's shopping. Nancy tried to slip in quietly, but one of her patients, Molly Draybach, saw her and squealed, "Doctor Nancy!" and caused Judy to interrupt her tale and let her small charges run around screaming for a while. Jaxson Moultree proudly displayed his healed lip but said he wished he still had the stitch because it was so awesome. "Now go back to Mrs. Stover's story, kids," Nancy said, "because I have to talk to Mrs. Gitchell."

There was only one person in the reading room. He looked up at her from behind a copy of *Entertainment Weekly*. Nancy had never met him but realized that, naturally, he would know her. Who didn't! She could not walk through this town without everyone knowing exactly who she was. In Chicago there were millions like her, millions, she thought, and how strange to find herself out here as the only one, not counting the old black man at the laundromat and two women in the high school cafeteria, but they went unremarked while she did not.

Susie was in her tiny office. "I can't bear the screeching out there," she said. "It's only on Saturday mornings. We never used to allow it, but Judy's doing her best."

"I'm afraid I caused the outburst."

"They do love you, Nancy. Take a seat."

There was barely room to squeeze into the metal folding chair beside Susie's cluttered desk, but when Nancy had unzipped her winter coat and unwrapped her scarf she told the librarian that she needed some advice. "We've done it," she began. "We're getting the judge's house." Susie Gitchell showed no surprise because word had undoubtedly already gotten around. "We have to wait for the will to be probated, but there don't seem to be any hitches and we have the key. We were thinking maybe you'd be willing, Susie—I know it's a lot to ask—but to come with us and look over Will Turley's library. The house is filled with books, and I mean filled, and we don't know what to do with them."

"I imagine it must be," said Susie as calm as a librarian would be. "When I was a girl I'd seen those heavy cartons he was carrying in, and that was just the start. And I remember when Henry Settle's father—that's Henry out in the reading room, he comes in Saturdays to keep up with the world, nice kid, he's the one who carried Mr. Turley to the hospital, as you probably know. Anyway, Henry's dad was a fine carpenter, but he was disabled too young. Anyway, he once went and built shelves for Mr. Turley. Last one of us to see inside that house. The judge used to have fancy parties. I recall as a girl seeing people dressed to the nines coming and going over there, but then not a soul for all these years. In winter from my bedroom window I could see through the bare branches of the maple that's just a stump now. I'd watch the Gales in that house and the Henshaws in yours and dream of being married to a romantic young rich man and living in one or the other some day. I couldn't decide which I'd prefer. The judge's house was grander, but the banker's looked cozier."

"We find it cozy," Nancy said. "We're quite at home there."

"Then why ever do you want to buy the judge's! Or is it true, Nancy, that Mr. Turley left it to you? That's what some people are saying and not just the small-minded ones."

Nancy wondered if confirming the rumor would be better or worse for their standing in Rockvale. Was it better to have money enough to buy or luck enough to be given? But she could not lie to Mrs. Gitchell. "Between you and me," she said knowing it would never stay secret, "he left it to us, and we don't know why, Susie, or what we're ever going to do with it. All those books! My husband thought maybe we could donate them as a kind of memorial collection to the library."

"I doubt we'd have the space."

"But maybe as an archive of sorts in the basement or housed over in the courthouse? They've got the county historical rooms upstairs."

"Truthfully, Nancy, it's not so much a matter of space as who'd bother to look at them. There might be a few volumes we could use. I'll come take a look, but there's not much call for the sorts of titles Will Turley collected."

"You read *Wuthering Heights*. Maybe some bookish girl in town—"

"I guess I got through it eventually. There's a copy here still, and *Jane Eyre* and some other famous ones—*David Copperfield, Moby Dick*, books every library should have. But Will Turley went in for absolutely everything, Nancy. There's not enough readers altogether in Sinnissippi County to read what that man read in his one lifetime. Nor would they care to. I'm only being realistic. And the cataloguing! You can't imagine what it takes me to get the new bestsellers out on the shelves."

"But we don't know what to do."

"Because you plan to rent the place out? No renter wants to look at shelves of old books. You renting it furnished?"

"We're not sure of anything—unfurnished probably. There's a few nice antiques. He lived so sparely. And we'd remove the shelves, except the judge's ones with glass doors. We could store the books in the basement, but they might get moldy. Mrs. Gitchell—Susie—it's an odd feeling I've been having that it's all up to us to take care of Will Turley's books."

"You've got the library bug," Susie Gitchell said leaning back as far as she could in the narrow space between her desk chair and the wall, where hung the sesquicentennial quilt depicting scenes of early days in the county—the pre-Civil War schoolhouse, the first farmstead, the house with the station on the Underground Railroad, the encampment of Chief Black Hawk's men down by the river where the Basswood Restaurant now stands. "I've lost the library bug myself," Susie said. "All I come here for now is the quiet and the magazines and some of the new books, I guess. Sam's got the TV blaring at home ever since he retired, so I need to get out of the house."

"But could you come look over the books anyway and maybe tell us what they are, because we're not sufficiently literary-minded. Our daughter could do it, but she's up at grad school."

"I'd like to see inside that house for sure, always wanted to. There might be a few titles we'd want, and maybe the high school will take some."

"But—" Nancy began, then did not know how to explain herself.

"I'll come by after we shoo out the little monsters."

"I don't want to appear ungrateful," said Nancy cautiously, "about you maybe taking some books, but I somehow feel we should keep them all together, I mean as Will's collection. It's probably foolish, or is it superstitious?"

"Because a dead man left them to you?"

"I'm not a superstitious person. I don't know what it is."

To Nancy the librarian suddenly looked like a weather-beaten Midwestern farmwife in some old movie on the black-and-white TV when she was little. "You can't hold onto things," Susie Gitchell said. "That bug can make life hell. Don't look so distressed, dear. Maybe the high school has a storage room. Talk to Principal Mack. He's more sentimental about books than I am."

There was some commotion out in the children's room then Judy Stover stuck her head in and said, "I'm done. It's just Henry in there still. I'm heading home."

"Thanks, Judy. Judy, you know Nancy Huggins."

"Sure do. Those kids love their Doctor Nancy." And off she went.

"Tell you what," Susie said. "I'll kick Henry out and we'll go look over those books, though really I'm only curious about the house."

Henry Settle offered to drop them off on his way, so they squeezed onto the seat of his truck, the very seat that had carried comatose William Turley to the hospital. The shy young man did not mention that fact, but both women knew it, everyone in town knew it. Henry's truck had acquired an heroic aura though it was only a rusty old Dodge. Nancy was pressed tight to Mrs. Gitchell's bony right hip and elbow and leaned herself against the door as far as she could.

"What did you learn from your reading today?" the librarian asked their chauffeur.

"Just catching up on the movies coming out."

"We don't get to see them here anymore. Henry, you're too young to remember the Star Theater."

"Over to the mall you can, but they sure cost. I just like keeping up on them, you know."

It was only a four-block ride, but it saved them an icy walk. Henry let them out in front of 19. No one said anything about 17, but Nancy caught Henry glancing across at Will's recently sanded front walk, so she tried to thank him with special warmth.

Because Susie Gitchell had never been inside the Henshaw house either, she was glad to come in first for a cup of tea. Nancy brewed a pot while Lawrence showed her around. "We bought it from the Merrills who bought it after Mrs. Henshaw died," he was saying out in the living room. "Did you know them?" And Nancy heard Susie say, "Didn't much like the Merrills. She was jittery and he was never home. You two are a great improvement." Nancy wondered if Susie had ever been inside a black family's home before. Most likely she had not.

"You've got it nicely fixed up, Mr. Huggins. My Sam would love that size of a TV. It's sunny here in the bay. I'd see Mrs. Henshaw sitting here in her chair doing her sewing when I lived across the street. I thought these two big old houses were just the ticket. Then I married Sam Gitchell. See, that's my old family bungalow across the street, the yellow one, and that stump was a great tall maple. I don't know how you keep a big place like this clean let alone heated."

Nancy served the tea, and when they warmed up and Lawrence was better acquainted with their guest, he suggested she bring Sam over on the first of February for the Super Bowl, but she said he seldom left his easy chair.

*****

Susie took it easy on the walk over and going up Will's front steps to the side porch. "Look at that," she said of the enameled oval with its nesting bird. "I never got to see it up close. It's a whippoorwill. See, it says so. He nailed that to his door when he moved in. I assumed it was his nameplate, but why would he have a nameplate when he never had a visitor?"

Lawrence slipped the key in the lock, and they were inside their other house.

"It's a library indeed, oh my!" Susie exclaimed. "What a wonder!" She stepped into the front parlor and then quickly to the back one. "Oh yes, the judge's shelves. I can imagine his leather-bound legal tomes. These old books of Will's seem a little shabby." And on into the dining room while Lawrence and Nancy waited between the parlors. "It's all Russians in here," came her voice, "this whole wall. Not in Russian, of course. Will Turley didn't read Russian or any other foreign language, I'm sure, but there's whole sets of Russian authors—Turgenev or however you say it and Dostoevsky and Tolstoy. Oh my, there were sets like these in the Rockvale library when I was a young volunteer. Who knows, these may be the very ones. No, not the Dostoevskys. Oh, the Chekhovs, yes, look, from the Rockvale Public Library, discarded July nineteen sixty-six. Will must've bought them at our rummage sale. Here's one I never heard of—Goncharov, *Oblomov*—Russian names always end with -ov or -sky, except Tolstoy. Oh. But then there's also Pushkin—"

"Lenin, Stalin," Lawrence called out. "Putin!"

"This is such fun," said Susie coming back to look over the judge's shelves. "It's like the Knighton College library my father took me to see for a special treat. Dad was a farmer's son. He didn't know much about books, but he knew how his daughter liked them. Now, the study, this is the English room. Look—Jane Austen, you see, *Pride and Prejudice* and all those, we still have them, nice editions, and then the Brontës— that's my Heathcliff—and Dickens and George Eliot—she was a woman, in fact, Nancy. I haven't seen books like these in years. Then Henry Fielding—and alphabetical by author. I can't even begin to have heard of them all. This is what we classify as literature, you see, it isn't popular fiction. I don't see poetry here, though. Will must've only liked novels, I guess, and short stories—of the literary sort. But here are all the Shakespeare plays, which we have, of course. And Robert Louis Stevenson. We have *The Strange Case of Dr. Jekyll and Mr. Hyde* and also *Treasure Island* in the children's room."

Lawrence had taken his wallet from his breast pocket and pulled out a scrap of paper. "Tell me," he said, "if you see *Is He Popenjoy?* by Anthony Trollope."

"What a funny title! Never heard of it. But here's the Ts, *Vanity Fair*, we still have that. I can't quite see through the glass. It's reflecting the sunlight. Here's your Trollopes, dozens of little blue books." She opened a door and picked one out. "No, that's called *The Fixed Period*. Hmm, *He Knew He Was Right*, another funny title. Oh, here's your book, Lawrence, in two volumes." She held them up for his inspection.

"I asked because—" But he remembered he had promised not to reveal how Eddie Boyce had snuck a peek in one of Mr. Turley's packages, so he improvised: "It's a title I heard of once."

"I didn't know you'd even heard of Anthony Trollope," said Nancy. "They did him on *Masterpiece Theatre*."

"And there's another book I was—thinking of."

"What's that you've got written down, Lawrence?"

"Just these books I've been curious about. *The Petty Bourgeois* by Honoré de Balzac."

"Now, Balzac would be French," said Susie. "These are all English. And look, this side of the room's Americans: *The Last of the Mohicans, The House of the Seven Gables*. And here's all these by Herman Melville. I didn't know he wrote so much else. And all these by Henry James! Edgar Allan Poe we've kept, of course. I see now what Will's got himself here. These are all the older authors. For instance, you don't see Ernest Hemingway or F. Scott Fitzgerald."

"They're probably upstairs," Nancy said, "where he has the paperbacks. He wanted his first floor to look elegant."

"But who'd see it besides him?" Lawrence wondered.

And Susie Gitchell said, "Maybe just elegant for himself, Mr. Huggins."

"Do call me Lawrence."

"Lawrence. But you're right, Nancy—the chandelier, the parquet, the carved wood, it's like a leather-bound book itself. I'd say you've got yourselves quite the house. My old girlhood dream—but I wouldn't touch it now, what with oil prices and the taxes."

"Have we made a foolish investment?"

"Not if you didn't have to pay for it," said Susie.

Lawrence got a nod from his wife, so he said, "Then you know about our old neighbor's generosity."

"It's puzzled us, Susie," Nancy said. "We only had him over for supper at most a dozen times."

"But you're the only folks who ever did."

"We were newcomers, we didn't know."

"Still, no one else ever tried."

"In all those years?"

"He didn't lend himself much to being invited," Susie said. "He never said anything back but 'how-de-do' and kept right on walking."

"But he stopped and stood there and talked with us out on the sidewalk," Lawrence said. "I wish I could reconstruct how that first meeting went. He must've said his 'how-de-do' and then we barged in with 'Hi, we're your new neighbors, Lawrence and Nancy Huggins from Chicago,' and so on until Nancy said to come over for supper. I doubt he said anything much at all. We were jackasses enough to keep yapping away at him."

"We even wondered," Nancy said, "to be totally honest about this, if it wasn't because we were African Americans and he didn't want to seem, I guess, rude."

Susie Gitchell had stepped into the front parlor's sunlight, which was shining through her thinning white hair and leaving her face in shade. "I'm so glad you said that, Nancy, I'm so glad. I couldn't have said it myself."

"You think that's what it was?"

"I couldn't be sure, but I'm so glad you said it. I don't know why people can't just mention things. This business of being black or white, or whatever else, is something we can't help noticing, isn't it, but then, so what!"

"That's the spirit," said Lawrence.

"Yet the small-minded so-called Christian folks think it's a very big what, and there's plenty of them around."

"We know there are," said Lawrence, and Nancy went and gave the librarian a soft hug.

"Oh, I feel better now," Susie said. "All I had to do was say what I think. Now what was that book you were looking for, Lawrence?"

"*The Petty Bourgeois*, by Honoré de Balzac."

"And that would be French, so let's see if it's in the front room—" She turned to the outside wall. "No, these are Germans. See, names like Hoffmann—I knew some Hoffmanns—Kleist, von Kleist, 'von' is German, and here's the man you pronounce like 'Gertie' though it looks like it 'Goth.' *Faust*—that's a drama not a novel. This side ends with Zweig. There was a Helen Zweig I used to know in town, made splendid apple pies. Ah, but see over on this side it starts again with the French. Oh my, look at all the Balzacs! *Lost Illusions* is the famous one I remember we had back when."

"These red books?"

"Why those in particular, Lawrence?" Nancy asked.

"I don't know. We're all petty bourgeois, aren't we?"

"We're surely not millionaires," his wife said with a quick elbow to his ribs, but he was already running his eyes along the spines until he found, in faded print, the words he had been searching for on two fat volumes. He pulled the first one off the shelf and carefully thumbed through its pages. The women had gone on to the next wall.

"These are the Greeks and Romans and then comes Italians," Susie said, "and here's Spanish, a big fat *Don Quixote*—we have the abridged version. And way down here, Ibsen's plays that used to be banned. If they could only see what was published today!"

The pages of the Balzacs were cut. Lawrence tried the second volume all the way to the end. At the foot of the very last page he saw a date written small in ink: August 13, 2004. These books had come into Eddie Boyce's post office from far Australia, and William Turley had cut the pages then read every one of them and recorded the date when he finished. Lawrence was sure he would also find a date on the last page of *Is He Popenjoy?*

"My, but you've got yourselves a wondrous old library here, Nancy," said Susie. "I doubt even Knighton College's is as complete as this. Of course, it's limited to literature, and too bad they're all such old editions."

Lawrence shut the book but carried it with him and followed them to the second floor, but he stopped on the landing and turned again to that last page and read to himself: "You are on the outside, my dear fellow, and you must be more content with your lot; governments come and go, societies perish or decay; but we dominate them all; the police is immortal!" *That's ominous*, he thought. And shouldn't it be "the police are immortal"?

"He couldn't have read all these," the librarian was saying pointing into the middle bedroom. "And just as you predicted, here's the twentieth century. You've got all the English in here—and the Irish. See?—George Bernard Shaw, James Joyce. Never heard of Dorothy Richardson, look at all of hers, and Virginia Woolf—I once tried but couldn't. And Americans on the other wall. What did I tell you! Willa Cather, I used to read her when I was young—nice big print, what beautiful grass-green books, aren't they? Sorry, I'm rattling on like a physic woodpecker! Here's your Fitzgeralds—and Sinclair Lewises, these orange and blues—and it keeps going down to Edith Wharton. Let's go see the front room."

There she found the famous Prousts and Manns. They were big names, she said, and there were more Russian-sounding ones— "Nabokov, oh dear," she said. They all meant something to Susie Gitchell from her library studies, but it bothered her terribly that there was no biography section or science and nature or history, and nowhere shelves of poetry. "Someone should come appraise it all, some book dealer," she said. "You might get something for the rare ones. They sell them on the Internet now. That's how Mr. Turley collected books in his later years, one by one from all over the world."

Nancy looked to Lawrence, who quickly said, "At the moment we'd like to try keeping it as a whole collection, that's how we're thinking. The appraisal's going to the real estate office for tax purposes. We'll see what it says."

"What usually happens," Susie said, "is dealers buy up a houseful for a lump sum then divvy it up later and toss out what they don't sell. We do that with our library sale. Some books just naturally end up at the dump."

Nancy grabbed Lawrence's elbow and squeezed, so he pulled her closer. "In here's his reading room, Susie," he said. "This is where he'd sit, the comfy chair and the wooden rocker depending on his mood, I guess."

She bent over to read the spine of the open book on the flat pillow. "*Private Papers*, hmm. But look, on this empty shelf, a pile by Kurt Vonnegut. We definitely have some of those. I think I heard he died recently. But these would be classified more as popular fiction. I wonder if Will had time to get to them before he died himself."

Lawrence casually picked up *Deadeye Dick* and found, below the last line, an inked-in date, April 8, 2008. "Any books by African Americans?" he asked.

"James Baldwin over here," said Susie. "And here we have *Invisible Man*, that one we have. No Toni Morrison, probably because she's not dead yet." She had to laugh. "What did Will Turley have about authors being dead?"

"Here's Zora Neale Hurston," said Nancy from the middle bedroom. "Our daughter Chloe got me to read a book of hers."

Susie had gone exploring down the hall. "Here's his little bedroom. Look how tidy he made his bed for the very last time! No books in here."

"Just one," Lawrence said, "by the bed, still wrapped in plastic. He must've been saving it."

"You know, Lawrence," said Susie, "I'm ashamed to say, most of what's out there I've never even heard of. Goes to show how much has been written. The pity is, who's ever going to want it all?"

Nancy called her in to see how clean his bathroom was, and after they had admired it she led her down the back stairs to inspect the kitchen where Susie exclaimed: "I'm so relieved! All these years I was afraid he lived in squalor, one of those quiet lonely men, you know, with stacks of trash everywhere. But he kept it tidy all by himself. That little Mexican fellow just took care of the outdoors."

"Puerto Rican," Nancy said.

"Well, if he'd only sanded the walk in time we'd still have our old Will who'd have gone on into his eighties, nineties even. See, you start thinking this way when you pass sixty-five."

"We're thinking that way at fifty-five," said Lawrence following them back through the dining room, with its wall of Russians, toward the front hall, but he stopped by the English shelves and opened the last glass door to find those little *Popenjoy* books, their spines not quite flush with the others after Susie had replaced them. Volume Two, last page, August 17, 2004. Four days later, half a volume a day. The last sentence: "Of Mr. Groschut it is only necessary to say that he is still at Pugsty, vexing the souls of his parishioners by Sabbatical denunciations." Another strange way to end a novel. Between the one about the police and now denunciations and Pugsty, and then what Will had been reading before he died about cooking potatoes with mint, Lawrence could not make sense of the man's personal taste in books. Perhaps he had no personal taste but simply read everything there was without question.

"What was that you said upstairs about a woodpecker, Susie?" Nancy asked when they opened the door and noticed the nesting whippoorwill on its enameled oval.

"Just something my old dad used to say when I got going too fast for him. He grew up on a farm."

AFTER CHURCH

hen the congregation had shaken hands with Pastor Miller and passed along through the double doors into the cold Sunday morning, Lawrence and Nancy stepped back inside to ask if they might have a private word.

"There's always time for that," said the small balding white man whose too-loose clerical collar made him look like a bobblehead doll, as Chloe had noted when she joined them once for a Sunday service. He was not an inspiring preacher, but Nancy knew he was a kind man who visited his hospitalized parishioners in genuine concern for their woes. He now led the Hugginses into his sunny little office beyond the cloak room. Rockvale Methodist was the oldest church in the county and had a spirit of good fellowship and sincere belief that appealed to Lawrence and Nancy, who were not drawn to rural Bible-thumping nor, in the other direction, to the Lutherans.

It did not take long to explain their present situation because Pastor Miller knew most of it already from the talk around town. The question that remained, as it remained for everyone, was what had they done for the old man to warrant his gift? When Lawrence explained they had not offered more than a dozen suppers and their own two pairs of ears, the minister said, "And two very good hearts as well. I don't say it to flatter. Mr. Turley had all his wits about him. He may not have known many actual people, but if, as you say, he read all those classic novels, he was well-versed in human nature. I suspect he was a fine judge of character. He was not, it seems, led by faith, but in his own way he studied the questions of love and redemption, and that's where our faith also leads us, isn't it?"

Seated side by side, Nancy and Lawrence nodded solemnly at the cheerful face across the desk where stood a clunky old Dell computer beside a pile of church bulletins.

"He came to trust you both as have, I may say, so many others in our congregation since you joined us. Aren't we lucky—"

"We're the lucky ones to have landed here in such a welcoming community," said Nancy.

"Let's say we're lucky all around," said Pastor Miller bobbing his head and smiling toothily. Then: "A will and testament is a sobering thing. Do you know why we call it a will and testament? It goes back to the Norman Invasion when England became, per force, a bilingual nation. Legal documents were written in two languages, so *will* is for the Anglo-Saxon speakers and *testament* for the French. *Will* means, what, *desire*? And *testament* refers to the head, the mind. I don't know if people a thousand years ago made quite the distinction we do between heart and head. In any case, lest I go on and on, let me simply suggest that Mr. Turley's head and heart led him to the same place, to the two of you, guardians for all he held dear, his house and his books. You mentioned a considerable legacy to a distant cousin, but your intuition is correct: money had little value to him but for its, shall I say, redemptive power, its power to be redeemed for volumes of literature—yes, and to keep him fed and housed, but his treasure, as you put it so well, Dr. Huggins, the treasure that you have inherited was indeed the most sacred thing for him: knowledge. I may regret his absence from any religious fellowship. I wouldn't begrudge the Roman Catholics if they could have solaced him, or he could have been a Quaker or a Jew, but you know, Lawrence and Nancy, if I may, he did find his own form of worship in his books. They may not have led him to Jesus Christ, but they must have succored him by teaching him truths. Secular truths may redeem us as sacred ones do. Of course, I'm not speaking of our redemption through Jesus Christ but of something that I trust helped him find peace in his earthly life. You're a banker, Mr. Huggins—Lawrence. At the county bank, people redeem checks every day, redeem their savings, and now it seems William Turley has written you, I might say, a check on a lifetime savings account in the form of his collection. I entirely appreciate your impulse, Nancy, not to sell it off piecemeal or give it away by lots but to hold it together as something in itself, a spiritual whole. It did save Mr. Turley. What would his life have been without it? You worry it's superstitious to feel you must honor his last wish. I wouldn't say so. If you were in financial straits, perhaps, but I assume that is not the case. What will the future bring? Any of us may slip on the ice. Will we leave gifts behind? Jesus Christ left us the gift of His life, and it would not be blasphemous of me to say that your old neighbor left you the gift of his. He himself evaporated into thin air on an icy winter's day, and what he left was his library." And here Pastor Miller paused.

"Is it anything the church might make use of—the house, I mean, better than we can?" Lawrence asked somewhat unsurely.

The pastor tilted his balding head in befuddlement.

"I mean as additional space—for an elder center or the Sunday school. I'm thinking aloud. We haven't talked this over."

"We couldn't possibly take on more space," said Pastor Miller, "though I much appreciate the thought. You'd be wiser to take in a tenant at an affordable rate, someone in need."

"Leaving all the books?"

"You were planning to ask Principal Mack if perhaps at the high school—I do like your notion of the William Turley Memorial Collection as a gift to the whole town."

"I was hoping to see Mr. Mack tomorrow," said Nancy.

"Or Knighton College over in Riparian County. They have quite a fine library. You'd feel so good knowing Mr. Turley's intellectual legacy was being preserved for others' use."

"But I have the terrible feeling," Nancy ventured to say, "that he left it just for us. That would've been crazy of him, wouldn't it?"

Pastor Miller laced his fingers together and gazed for a moment in thought at the ceiling. "I believe, if it's any comfort, that he left you his books because he trusted you to find them their next proper home. True, he placed a burden upon you, but behold, his burden is light, to paraphrase Matthew. You will do only the best you can. In time, someone will undoubtedly borrow a book and not return it, or lose it, or a future librarian will separate the sheep from the goats or winnow the wheat from the chaff or box it all in a storeroom never to see the light of day again. There's no assurance, no Federal Deposit Insurance Corporation, so to speak, but you'll have done all that two good-hearted people can do. Leave the rest to God."

"So we should only try our best?" Nancy asked. "I've been so restless, pastor, ever since we were told of the inheritance. I've felt we owed him something."

"We all of us owe each other," Pastor Miller said. "You two have understood that better than most. It's what makes you good people. You took the lonesome old man into your house and fed him when no one else had."

"He wouldn't go to anyone else," said Lawrence.

"It was as if he chose us," said Nancy.

"Speaking of being fed," the minister said in a brighter tone, "the missus will want me home shortly. I trust I've been of some help. Life presents its mysteries, and we are not given to understand them perfectly. I know you will find contentment knowing you have already done the charitable good deed and only this last little piece remains, something like a service for the dead. You notice I'm given to double meanings. To do a service—I don't believe there was one for Mr. Turley, was there? I'm told a funeral home took the body and no one here knows where it was to be laid to rest. But it was merely his body. You both have his books, which I may say are both his heart and his mind."

Pastor Miller stood up smilingly pleased with his counseling, Nancy could tell. But she realized on their walk home that they had omitted something important and so said to her husband, "He couldn't have truly helped us."

"I think he did."

"No, honey, you told him about all the money for the cousin, but I never told him about Will's terrible scars. How could Pastor Miller help us without knowing that?"

"It was so private to Will. It wouldn't have been right to tell him. We would never even have known if—"

"But, Lawrence, it's still haunting me. I keep thinking of old Will sitting up in his chair reading for all those years with his back and chest covered in scars. Maybe they didn't hurt anymore, but they were there, along with the books he was holding in his hands and reading aloud to himself in his empty house. I can't help not wanting to let a single book go, every one he ever held. I should've explained that to the pastor. Is it because I treat so many sick children?"

"It's better we didn't tell him," Lawrence insisted.

"But that meant he couldn't give us the best advice." Then, noting her husband's knotted eyebrows under his fur hat, Nancy took his arm as they walked and said, "Don't worry, I'll still go tomorrow and see the principal on my lunch break." The nicest thing since Will died, she told herself, was how she and Lawrence had grown closer. Even when they argued it soon came out all right. Even their lovemaking lasted longer and was more tender.

"I think he did read every single book, Nancy. I didn't tell you. I looked at the last pages of several, and he'd written down the dates when he finished them. I'd been trying to calculate how many books he'd have to read a week, and it came out to three or four, if he was to have read them all. There were probably a few unfinished, the one about cooking potatoes, obviously, and the newest arrivals, but I bet we'll find most every book over there has some date at the very end written small and neatly in ink."

AT THE SCHOOL

They had spent a lovely quiet Sunday afternoon with no TV football and the two of them together—and then a long nap and a sense of calm from having talked with their pastor, yet in the morning at breakfast and, later, busy at work, Nancy did not sense any diminution of her restlessness. The burden of inheritance still weighed on her. All Pastor Miller had said amounted simply to "do the best you can."

At lunchtime she drove out to the high school on the other side of town. Antonius Mack was a tall craggy man from a family that had been in the county since the settlement. Having once served on a hospital committee together, he and Nancy were glad to see each other. She was determined not to reveal her ambivalence but to state her mission straightforwardly. "Antonius," she said taking an adjacent armchair in the teachers' lounge where he had brought her for coffee, "we're now to own, along with his house, the wonderful collection of Will Turley's books that we'd prefer to donate to the high school, if you could see a way to accept them as a whole. To witness how one man had done so much reading might be an inspiration to the students."

The principal tossed his gray head back with a guffaw. "Oh dear, I'm sorry, Nancy, but Will Turley—an inspiration!"

"I only meant his reading. For the more gifted kids—"

"Oh dear, Nancy." He took her hand, the one not holding the coffee mug, and turned serious. "I love books as much as the next guy, but it's difficult enough getting them to read the books we have. You should see our storeroom—old readers and workbooks and paperbacks from years past, all marked up and dog-eared, and they're put off when we plop them on their desks. Either they want their own fresh copies to mark up or they want to read the assignment online. There's whole anthologies called *Great American Short Stories* they can download for free now. They love it. They can annotate or highlight right on the screen, and the younger teachers like to set up chat rooms for class discussions. Now I'm talking about our motivated kids, the gifted ones, as you call them. But the others don't want to feel out of it, so even they will try. We're keeping up with things out here."

"Still, to see the actual books—"

"We do have a decent little library here," Principal Mack said, "and they've all been to the public library at some point in elementary school. How many books did it turn out old Turley owned?"

"We haven't counted, but my husband estimated it's close to ten thousand."

"Ten thousand!"

"And they're all literature—you know, short stories and novels and plays—and what's amazing, Antonius, is that he'd read most all of them. That's what I meant about inspiration."

"Nancy, oh, I love you. You're so hopeful! It's what makes you a great pediatrician. But I tell you, if we took the honors English kids to see ten thousand books all read by one single man, they'd think he was a totally weird dude. And that's the motivated ones. It could actually prove counterproductive. But show them on the Internet how they can get any book ever written anytime from anywhere, that'll get 'em! In effect, they each own ten thousand books already that don't take up any space. Am I sounding ungrateful? Oh, Nancy, it's so touching that you thought of us."

"No, no," she said, "I know it's all online, but I thought, for kids to see it here in the flesh, might still be something."

"His books must mostly be quite old," Antonius Mack said. "He showed up in Rockvale in the fifties—I don't remember the year, I was only just born—but growing up I'd see him around town. Even back then, rumor was he had more books than the public library."

"You remember him as a young man?"

"I was one of the studious little kids. He seemed old then, but I suppose he was still in his thirties. He was big, not tough or strong but sort of a big bear, not fearsome though. He was soft the way bears would look if you didn't know they were dangerous. And he didn't come across at all crazy. You should ask Susie Gitchell about him. She probably talked to him more than anyone before you and your husband came to town. Maybe she'd have use for some of his books."

"She came with us to look at them, but the library doesn't have the space, she said, and there's not enough call for Will's sorts of books."

"Oh, Nancy, you came in like Lady Bountiful, and now I'm sending you away a supplicant who's been denied. I feel so bad."

Nancy smiled as cheerfully as she could. Antonius Mack meant well. He was a friendly man who belonged here. "You grew up in Rockvale, didn't you," she said, "and your parents did, and their parents—"

"All the way back to the county's first schoolmaster, I'm proud to say."

"And you've devoted yourself to the kids here."

"You've done so, too, now, Nancy." He took her free hand again in his long pale fingers and held on.

She took a long sip of her cooling coffee then said, "I suppose it's the same back in Chicago. We left early in two thousand seven, and it was looking bad then. The last thing those schools need is Will Turley's books. I don't know your politics, Antonius, but being in education you must worry about it the way I do about health care. Can I say something personal? It sounds strange even to me, but when we found the old man next door had left us his house—you've heard that's how it was, everyone seems to know—" The principal nodded and let her hand drop though she scarcely noticed. "But when we went inside the house and saw the books—we also knew he had lots of books, but to see ten thousand books all in one man's house was something we couldn't have imagined—well, it put a giant weight on us. I felt—Lawrence did too—we felt we were being called to do something and not only for ourselves."

"In terms of pounds alone," Antonius Mack said, "books do certainly weigh. Library floors have to be shored up with heavy beams to hold that much weight. The kids' new libraries I'm talking about are light as a bird. They're accessible at any computer terminal. And they're coming out with little gizmos for any kid to carry ten thousand books in a backpack. Of course, it's not only the physical weight you're feeling. I grew up with old books. My family, going back generations, loved books. I still have books from when my great-great-great-grandfather was schoolmaster. His name's inscribed in each with a date, eighteen forty-something. Now that's old! Were you talking about that kind of weight, the weight of the past?"

Nancy thought and thought. She had not thought of it as the past, but maybe it was.

"The past takes up too much space," the gray-headed white man said crossing his long legs at the knee and leaning toward her. "In our hearts, I mean." Nancy looked into the dark brown eyes staring at her like some prophet. "But meanwhile," he said with a soft chuckle, "you're stuck with a houseful of musty old volumes."

"We may try the college library," Nancy said.

"Good thought. They've got memorial thises and memorial thats over there. They'd evaluate it and you could take a tax deduction for the donation. My sister wants me to donate our old family books to the county archives, but she'll have to wait 'til I'm dead. It's only one shelf, probably not worth all that much, but I'm a romantic. Do you realize what owning a shelf of books would've meant out here on the frontier before the Civil War? In one sense, that schoolmaster was a wealthy man."

"All Will Turley's shelves—" Nancy began.

"But it's not his books," said Principal Mack, "it's what in them that we're teaching our kids. Or trying to. Besides, literature's only one part of it. There's so much else out there to be learned. You studied medicine, your husband studied finance."

"Our daughter's getting a doctorate in literature," Nancy said with some pride. "She's at Lawrence University in Wisconsin. They already have her teaching a course for freshmen up there."

"Then maybe she'll know what to do with your books. I call them yours even if you haven't read any yet."

"I've read maybe a few on Chloe's recommendation," Nancy said, but now she had to get back to her patients.

At the College

efore bed that night, Lawrence had agreed to go try the college library next. Nancy was so dispirited she was glad to hand over the task, and Lawrence had a morning meeting at AmTrust-Riparian anyway.

"But we're donating the whole collection, remember. They have to take it all. I don't want to hear if they plan to throw half of it out or sell it off to dealers. Still, maybe if we just never knew—am I being unreasonable?"

"It's the accountant in me," Lawrence said, "but I'd get itchy if they only kept, say, volumes one, five, and nine of something. A full set's a full set! Maybe I'm unreasonable too. And it makes me mad that our own library and school won't take Will's books. We should maybe call up Tuskegee or Howard or some poor small black college in the South to see if they don't want them, but they'd probably say the same damn thing."

Now after they had set their bedtime paperbacks on their nightstands—his thriller, her mystery—and the two of them were lying there propped up on pillows before they turned out the lights, hardly ready for sleep, Nancy perceived a nervous flickering of Lawrence's eyelids. "You're worried about the bank," she said, "that's part of it." She knew he kept his anxieties to himself and had long ago learned when to let him know she knew. It did not help to ask questions or offer support when trouble was looming. He would be fine once he could do something but not when he was waiting for something to happen. "Your AmTrust meeting tomorrow?"

"What's funny," he said, "is my position's safer out here than if we'd stayed in the city. That's where cuts are coming. They won't be reorganizing a little branch like Sinnissippi. And the feds are working on it, Nancy. Have faith. We'll weather it, don't fret."

"I'm not the one fretting," she said, but that was as far as she took it. She would see how he felt tomorrow evening.

And, in fact, the next noon Lawrence found himself pulling out of the Riparian branch's parking lot in a much lighter mood. Rose Carron and their fellow managers from Freeport, Mount Carroll, Galena, and Dixon had teleconferenced with Chicago and been assured nothing in northwestern Illinois would change. Secretary Geithner was developing a stabilization program, and the president would have another stimulus package on the way. Congress would put it through despite what some Republicans needed to say to certain constituents. After all, they own the banks, Lawrence told himself as he drove happily toward Knighton College, facts and figures still rushing through his head. He realized how his worry over Will Turley's books had kept his mind off his real worries. Giving away ten thousand books was small potatoes. Potatoes—why did the last paragraph Will ever read have to be about potatoes! Lawrence had always liked to think of him reading histories and philosophical treatises and books on science or maybe even economics. No doubt his novels were famous books by great authors but with no practical information in them. Yet Will gave the impression of having known so much.

Lawrence drove along the narrow river that separated the county seat from the college. Despite a cold wind, some undergrads were jogging past in sweatsuits. As he crossed the bridge, he had a sudden vision of Michelle Obama out there striding beside his Honda Civic. In recent days she had often popped into his head. On TV when they said the first lady did such-and-such or the first lady's dress was designed by so-and-so and he saw her there on the big screen, it gave him a feeling even beyond what he had for the president. He had somehow been prepared for him but not for her or for their daughters, black girls from Chicago, but there they were, the first family. It must have something to do with how much he loved Nancy and Chloe.

He followed the wooden signposts to the library. Parking spaces were scarce, but he eventually found one and walked back on a well-shoveled pathway toward the handsome old brick building with limestone pillars. "W. Ansel Stark Memorial Library" was emblazoned across the cornice. Young people were sloping up and down the steps, more people of color than he had seen since their last trip down to Dixon for the barber and hairdresser. There were Asian faces, Latin ones, a few black kids, too, but plenty of whites.

Lawrence had an appointment with the acquisitions librarian at 12:30 and was astonished to find her a young black woman with a shaven head, huge earrings, and a colorful knit shawl draped across her shoulders.

"Mr. Huggins, I'm Barbara Chriss, do come in."

Lawrence hoped his eyes had not betrayed his readjusted expectation. She was likely as surprised by him but showed no sign in her relaxed manner. Perhaps she had Googled him.

"So you're at AmTrust. That's my bank," she said.

"The Rockvale branch, but my wife and I are Chicagoans. We've only been out here two years."

"St. Louis," Ms. Chriss said of herself, "but came up to school, managed to stay on."

"Our daughter's in grad school in Wisconsin."

"Madison?"

"Lawrence University. Named after her dad," he joked but then explained, "My Christian name's Lawrence."

The young woman did not appear to respond to his humor but quickly said, "So—a collection of old books?"

In Chicago it would be nothing to speak professionally with another African American. Here it almost called for some acknowledgment, but Lawrence simply answered her question. "The gentleman who left them to us kept buying books through his entire life. Some are quite new. He wasn't into living authors, but he must've watched for them to die so he could start in on them too. He was an eccentric, but we do miss him."

Ms. Chriss took all this in, as if she had heard similar tales before. "Black writers?"

Ah, good, thought Lawrence. "Yes, there are," he said, "and many women, but it's pretty much all literature books only. He had a lot of complete matched sets. I estimated maybe ten thousand individual volumes."

At last, Ms. Chriss showed some surprise, beringed fingers to her lips and eyebrows raised to her shaved scalp. Lawrence was still not used to the look, and it was apparently what Chloe's Deet also affected. Ms. Chriss said slowly, "Literature—hmm. We have an extensive collection from before the First World War, but perhaps some single titles—the problem is that for important texts there are new authoritative editions. As for foreign literatures—I assume yours are all in English?—recent translations supersede the inaccurate or sanitized old ones. Especially from French. I was a French major. Spent my junior year in Côte d'Ivoire."

"My wife and I feel—" Lawrence began but then changed tack. "So older editions would not be valuable for scholars?"

"Perhaps at a larger university, but we're just a liberal arts college. Your daughter should ask them up at Lawrence, but my sense is that universities either have the old editions or are gradually replacing them. As I say, there may be single titles, but we're not equipped to take on a collection of that size. Personnel hours alone—and shelf space. Very generous offer, though."

"Generosity—" Lawrence said but stopped to consider. Then he asked as politely as he could, "Is it generous if no one wants what you're giving?" He did not want to sound sour to this stylish young woman, so he quickly said, "Maybe one of the traditionally black colleges would take an interest."

"I'll be honest with you, Mr. Huggins. Sort of doubt it. There's such a number of alums who want to donate from their grandparents' or parents' libraries or even from their own, and we generally have to accept to keep the alumni base connected. I suspect it's the same at Howard, say, and yours wouldn't really be the sorts of books a black college looks for right now, not as a collection anyway. If you put an inventory online, they might perhaps pick and choose, but with the time it would take and the shipping costs—"

Lawrence was sinking back into the overcoat he had unbuttoned but not taken off. "I suppose we're saddled with a burden we don't quite know how to carry," he said almost to himself but then, looking up into Barbara Chriss's dark eyes, said, "It's as if the old gentleman left us his heart and soul. We feel we must somehow keep his collection intact."

"One other possibility is to approach a book dealer, but not if you want to preserve the integrity of—but why exactly would you?"

Lawrence sat up straighter and tried to match the handsome young woman's wide bright smile shining at him from between the large hoops in her ears. He wished Chloe were there to do the talking. She must know women like this Barbara Chriss. "It would be cold-hearted," he said, "to take one book here and one book there. I'm not much of a novel reader. I'd hoped for some nonfiction in his house. I do read a lot in my own field and other subjects I care about, histories and biographies, and our daughter's introduced us to some Caribbean and African writers, but they're mostly still alive."

"Maybe there's some mad collector out there on eBay," Ms. Chriss suggested. "Could be fronting for a dealer, though. Can never be sure."

"If my wife didn't find out—"

"Aha, she's the sentimentalist!"

Lawrence's impulse was to stand up for Nancy. With a firm shake of his head, he resolved himself. "No, I'm afraid it's me, too. We're old-fashioned, I guess. I grew up being taught you didn't ever mess with a book, no book of any sort, not just the Bible. My old cousin Gertrude who raised me had great respect for words on a page."

"But, Mr. Huggins, words don't have to be on pages anymore. In libraries we know that, more than anyone. We're here to preserve words, aren't we? Words are indestructible now. That's the good news. First they went by mouth, then by the written hand, then by printing press, but now they'll be everywhere and always. In the smallest African village! We do love our books, we continue to purchase, they're a pleasant way to read, but even that's changing. Don't worry, words are safe now forever, Mr. Huggins. They won't ever go out of print again."

A thought struck Lawrence with sudden force. "When we went into our neighbor's house for the second time," he said, "just to see all those books sent chills through me. The first time they seemed like too many damn books, but by the second time we'd learned what the old gentleman had suffered and could imagine what collecting those books must've meant to him."

"He had a long illness?"

"No," Lawrence said, "his old age was quite healthy. I meant what he'd suffered back in his youth."

Barbara Chriss had leaned forward with concern in her large eyes and wrapped her colorful shawl tighter about her shoulders, but

Lawrence knew now how Nancy had felt talking to Principal Mack, so he stood and politely offered his thanks with a formal handshake and departed.

He walked slowly to his car, passing silent students in their headphone worlds and others talking loudly on cellphones. None looked over at him. He beeped the lock and saw the tail lights flash, but when he was seated inside he did not turn the key. He sat. He was in danger of crying. He almost wished his tears would burst forth, despite himself, but they only began to well up and then drip onto his cheeks. He was crying for Nancy's sake. She had only wanted to please Will once more as she had pleased him before with her home cooking. She had wanted to make up for all his scars, as if Will Turley were now watching them from above and would be glad of what they were trying to accomplish. They did not believe in the heaven of their grandparents, where the dead watched over the living and judged them, nor did they believe in the heaven of their parents, where the dead were reborn in a better place with all their tears wiped away. Nancy and Lawrence's heaven was a collection of souls with their mortal shortcomings dispelled and the residue a goodly essence of the kindnesses and wisdom their once embodied selves had striven to be worthy of. "That's worthy of heaven," big sisterly cousin Trudy used to say when little Lawrence did something she highly approved of. And to reprimand him she would say, "That's behavior unworthy of heaven, Lawr. You know better than that." When he first met Nancy Sublette, Lawrence knew right away how worthy of heaven she was and knew how lucky he was to have found her out of the millions in that city. It was why he was crying now, thinking of his Nancy and their Chloe while all those college students shuffled past in their boots and parkas with their backpacks and electronics.

He had to hurry back to the bank. First, he took out his own cellphone and called the hospital to tell Nancy of his failure at the college library. She said she had a notion it would turn out like that and had already decided they must do something else. That evening they must go into the other house and, being there again, try to understand William Turley anew. Lawrence wondered how that could help, but Nancy was convinced it would.

UNDER THE MATTRESS

After supper, as they bundled themselves up again, Lawrence said, "Why does it always feel colder out here in Rockvale than back in the city?"

"It does? Maybe it's from the houses being farther apart."

"But winds off the lake and roaring between the tall buildings—"

"It's psychological. We're more alone out here. Nature's closer and takes up more space with wind and snow."

"I was remembering Thanksgiving at your sister's last time we were home."

"That's two months ago, so of course it was warmer," Nancy said.

While they crunched over the hard-packed snow toward the dark house, she also thought of her oldest sister Martha's house in Andersonville where they had all gathered, the Hugginses, too. Nancy and Lawrence and Chloe heard firsthand the tales of Grant Park and saw Martha's big grandson Brian's pictures on his laptop of the tiny waving Obamas over the heads of the crowd while Martha and Laura prepared things in the kitchen. Having two so much older sisters had accustomed Nancy to being doted on the way Lawrence had been by Gertrude Huggins. She had often thought they were just two pampered kids who somehow found each other, though she was already in med school and he was beginning at the bank. And they went off in a different direction from the other Sublettes and Hugginses, even when they lived nearby. It was the downside of their better educations. Now they may have gone too far, but home would still always be home, Nancy thought as she climbed Will Turley's steps behind her husband.

Felipe Reyes must have been by again to sprinkle salt pellets and scrape off what ice he could. Lawrence unlocked the door, and they were soon inside. He flicked the switch by the door, and Nancy went straight to the thermostat in the stairwell. "Let's see what it's like when it's warm! It's at fifty. I'll put it to sixty-five. I wonder what Will set it at." They heard a comforting hum rise from the cellar they had yet to inspect.

"I don't imagine he stinted himself on heat with his kind of money," Lawrence said flicking switches in the parlors. The ceiling lights were refitted gas fixtures, not real chandeliers, the realtor woman had explained, and their plaster medallions were particularly lovely, she said, but was there a market for a house this grand in Sinnissippi County? Perhaps some professor would take an interest despite the long commute. She kept up her chatter, but the two of them had paid little attention. They could tell she was angling for them to resell through her and did not like being pressured. But it was a possibility, Nancy decided when she saw those book-lined rooms again and said, "It seems even emptier this time."

"I was thinking it seemed more homey," said Lawrence.

"Homey!"

"This time the books don't look as orphaned. When we came with Mrs. Gitchell I could only think of Will not being here to appreciate them anymore. It gave me a chill."

"But then we were still thinking we'd find them a new home."

"I fear this is their home," Lawrence said. "We may have to keep them, after all." He was standing by the German shelves and pulled out a book at random. "*The Poggenpohl Family*. What the hell is that! Hmm, University of Chicago Press, I'll be damned. We'll never read any of these kinds of books, and they're going to belong to us as soon as probate's done. In fact, they already do belong to us. I called Rod Strite this afternoon to check on things, and he says as soon as someone dies the heirs take possession from that very moment but don't know it for sure until the court 'accepts the will.' Once it does, possession's retroactive to the moment of death, Strite says, so this has already been ours for nearly a month, and here I'd been thinking of it in a kind of limbo. Strite put it this way: legally, a thing can never not be owned by someone. He's such an upbeat kid. He loves that job of his. I did get him to admit he'd been less certain before John Lee's letter came. 'Yeah, Mr. Huggins, you got me,' he said. So I said, 'Nice bluffing, Rod.' I like him. We should ask him to redraw our own wills with our new property." Lawrence shut the slim little book he had forgotten he was holding and tucked it back on its shelf.

"It still feels emptier in here to me," Nancy said. She cast her eyes around both parlors then headed through the dining room of Russian books to the kitchen to look over the cans and jars in the cupboards. "We've got to figure out who Will really was, Lawrence."

"How will that help us decide what to do?"

"There's spaghetti sauces and chili con carne and canned peaches and pears in here. Let's see—unopened peanut butter, noodles, bars of dark chocolate. He didn't eat very well. We should've fed him more often. All these soup cans and dried soup packets and bouillon cubes—I guess he ate lots of soup. Red Rose tea, no coffee, Carnation powdered milk—"

"Honey, I don't think this helps."

"But the realtors took the perishables. I hope he ate fruits and vegetables and some meat, for heaven's sake, for protein. Maybe the fridge was full before they unplugged it. What about the drawers?"

"Napkins, dime-store cutlery."

"There isn't anything nice."

"Those old Victorian pitchers and what-not in the dining room. All he needed was a few plates and bowls and the pans on the stove. Nice things wouldn't have made much difference to him or he'd have had them. He had enough money. Maybe he kept the thermostat low anyway."

"Oh, I hope not," said Nancy heading toward the back hall where she pulled a string to light their way down to the cellar, but when she pulled another string at the bottom, all they saw was an aged washer and dryer and the old furnace puffing away, blowing warm air up through the metal ducts.

"It must need a new filter. We'll have it checked out," Lawrence said. "Look at the old fusebox. We'll have to update the systems."

"Oh, look!" Nancy had opened the dryer and pulled out a pile of laundry. "Clean white sheets, pairs of long johns twisted up—oh, Lawrence, his old man long johns! And quilted undershirts and his thick white socks. And a gray flannel shirt—I can see him wearing it. And the khakis he always wore! Honey, he'd just done his laundry, and upstairs he'd made his bed fresh. His last laundry!" Tears were hovering behind her eyelids again. "I should fold them and take them upstairs."

"But leave them for now," said Lawrence.

She piled the laundry on top of the dryer and said, "At least it's bone-dry down here, and there's nothing stored. It's all swept clean, no cobwebs. We could bring the books down if we rent the house out. We could hire Henry Settle to dismantle the shelves and set them up along these walls and run a dehumidifier to be safe."

"Now you're being practical."

"I suppose we'll have to be."

They turned off the lights and went on up the back stairs to the second floor. Nancy opened the medicine cabinet above the bathroom sink. "Old straight razor and shaving brush—look, some Extra Strength Tylenol, oh dear, and Oxycodone prescribed by Artie Pratt, 'take as needed for pain.' That worries me. It's still mostly full. Perhaps the pain wasn't often severe. Who knows, he may have had internal injuries, not just the scars. But Artie would've said. Probably plain old-age aches—"

"Bath towels neatly folded," said Lawrence, "sticky shampoo bottle, no shower on this old tub. I bet he took long hot baths to soothe those aches and pains. He may not have had nice utensils and dishes, but I bet he kept the house toasty and took long hot baths. Let's grant him that."

Nancy had stepped into the bedroom. "He must've made his bed with clean sheets that very morning. Look how smooth the pillowcase is. He hadn't rested his head there yet. It was waiting for him. It all makes me so sad."

She turned to leave the room, but Lawrence had opened the closet door and found several pairs of identical khaki pants and flannel shirts in various shades—brown and gray and green and dark blue—and some short-sleeved plaid shirts. "All in order," he said, "summer and winter." He pulled open the top dresser drawer. "Will only wore white cotton socks, remember? Two pair here, the rest in the laundry—and the pair he was wearing that day." In the middle drawer Lawrence found sleeveless white undershirts and one more long-sleeved quilted one and, in the bottom drawer, the same seasonal distinction: one more pair of long johns and a stack of white boxer shorts. "He never had to think what to wear, and he'd do laundry once a week, Monday mornings. He died on a Monday afternoon."

Nancy was watching from the doorway, but Lawrence could tell she wanted him to stop talking.

"I'm sorry, honey, I thought you wanted to try to understand him."

"It's hard, though," she said. "I can see him dressing quickly and vacuuming and dusting and having a quick bite to eat, just to be able to spend more time with his reading. But Susie told me he once used to go outside and tend his garden."

"When he was young," said Lawrence. "He must've wanted the property to look good to the town. He wasn't a man to live in a ramshackle house overgrown with weeds and vines. That's why he hired Felipe. He had his pride."

"By the bed, there's nothing but that book? Is the floor all swept clean underneath too?"

Lawrence knelt down and saw only shadowy floorboards with light falling on the far side from the ceiling light. "Not a dust bunny. You know, back when I was a boy I'd stash the mash notes I got from girls under my mattress."

"Oh, Lawrence!"

"Maybe Trudy snooped, but she never said so." He reached his hand under the tightly tucked woolen blanket and felt around.

"Lawrence, don't!"

Then he touched some paper and looked up in surprise at his wife's shaking head.

"No!" she said.

But he carefully drew out a large manila envelope creased by the bedsprings. "No? But you wanted to find—" He stood up and passed it to her reluctant hand.

"I don't know, oh dear, he even hid it from himself. And it looks very old," Nancy said turning the envelope over to trace the rusty tracks of the bedsprings. "Maybe he put it there years ago and forgot about it."

"I wonder what it could be," Lawrence said. "Will Turley slept above it every night. From the marks it seems it hasn't ever been moved."

"It may be ours now, but I don't want us to open it."

"Then we'll take it home and think it over."

"Or put it right back? Just for now, honey. Please. It must be very private."

"No," Lawrence said, "we'd better take it home. Aren't you curious?"

"And here it was me who hoped we'd understand Will better simply by being over here," Nancy said. "I thought we'd maybe get an inkling of what he'd want us to do about his books." She handed the manila envelope back and quickly headed down the hall toward the light in the front stairwell as if in fear of being caught trespassing.

Lawrence flicked off the bedroom light and tucked the envelope under his arm. "Set the thermostat back down to fifty," he called after her. When he reached the bottom stair they both heard the furnace below them shut itself off. "I bet he kept the house warm," Lawrence said, "not so much for himself as for his books, to protect them from the dank and damp." But Nancy was already out the front door.

*****

At home they settled themselves down with cups of hot chocolate and cozied up side by side on the sofa where, despite Nancy's trepidation, Lawrence managed to convince her to let him pull out from the envelope a set of yellowed letters, once folded in thirds but long since flattened out, one handwritten page each, and all signed "Love, Dad." The first was dated June 26, 1955—"The week I was born," said Lawrence—and the dates continued two or three a year till 1969, a stack of some thirty letters in a good draftsman's fountain pen script.

Lawrence read the top one carefully to himself then passed it on to Nancy, who had leaned her head on his sweatered shoulder, afraid of what they might soon learn. In silence the yellowed sheets of paper passed from him to her, and this is what they each read in turn:

> Dear Son,
>
> We both miss you sorely, but you must be gentler with your mother. It would be best if you did not go into details. She's all right as long as she doesn't have to think

about it anymore. I am better able to absorb what has happened. Although I was too young for the first war and too old for the second, I've played enough sport in my day and hunted and fished with my compadres, and also in my work I've seen plenty of that side of men's natures. We can be a cruel lot, men can. I am sorry you feel the need to retreat from us for a time, but I fully understand. Perhaps it's preferable. I'm thinking of your mother's sake. She ought not to dwell on such things. It is painful for her to have learned such troubling things of the son she had been so confident of. But she truly misses you. We will patiently await a visit when you feel ready and meanwhile will not intrude. Strange as the circumstances may be, we are pleased you now have no financial worries. Keep us in your thoughts.

Love, Dad

Dear Son,

We are doing well. Your mother does not go out much, but she's content at home reading and keeping house. I'm considering an early retirement to keep her better company but have yet to make a decision. My work, your mother says, is what matters to me. It distresses her that now you will not have to work. She has a distaste for idleness in men and resents C. P. all the more for that bequest. To her mind it is an added insult. But I take money more seriously than she does. I know how much of it is needed to live as we do. That's why I have worked so hard to make it. I would rather have spent more of my life fishing at Tahquamenon. Suburban life is not for me the way it is for my sister Lily and her good Republican John and your unloved cousin John Junior. No doubt you are glad to be out of their orbit. With our parents gone, Lily Turley Lee with her birdsong name is quite the grande dame of the village and will not let your mother forget it. We see them all too often. Sometimes I envy you your hermitage. Would it be spoiled if you just once came to visit us? It's been a full year. Your mother will manage better now, I think. But give us fair warning.

Love, Dad

After reading the second letter Nancy whispered, "What's Tahquamenon?" but Lawrence had no idea and only shrugged.

"It's C. P., though, who left him the insurance," he said. "That's Caleb Pitchley."

They each read on, Nancy one letter behind, and she held onto Lawrence's forearm and squeezed tight when a phrase particularly touched her.

Dear Son,

We are largely back to normal, if I may call what we have normal in any normal sense. What is normal? I have come to understand that there is no normal in family life. John and Lily consider themselves the epitome of normal and expect everyone to follow their example. Meanwhile, John Junior cavorts like a wildcat and leaves his women as soon as he captures them. And he's already turned thirty! I know he was an unfortunate presence in your childhood. If only you'd had a sister, a younger sister would have been best. She would have taught you how to take care of a woman. My grand older sister never took much care of me, and I admit it is only through my bank account that I manage to care properly now of your mother. I had hoped your visit would have comforted her. I did not foresee the look in her eyes when she saw you again. I'm sure it was as painful for you. In our way we did get through it, but it did not accomplish what I had hoped. Shall we wait awhile and then try again? I agonize about her. If I were to retire and stay closer to home, I could perhaps moderate her moods. Yet what would I do here all day? I'm a mild man as long as I have plenty to occupy myself in the city, but I can't rely on the occasional hunting trip to keep my sanity. I'm only fifty-five! I'm not done yet. Neither are you, though you take after your mother more than you've ever taken after me. I will leave it at that.

Love, Dad

Dear Son,

I must tell you that I have located your country lawyer, Mr. Elmer Sturtevant, who reports well of you. He calls you a fine young man and says you've settled in a solid old house, and your substantial trust, he tells me, will come to your parents in the remote case of you predeceasing us. He does not have your street address, he claims, only this post box and no telephone number, says you have none. I also finally contacted your Mr. Bell, who was even less forthcoming. His duty is to look after your funds, which he's more than capable of doing (he has a first-rate reputation in Chicago) but he would reveal no particulars, as is no doubt proper. "That's between your son and me" was all he would say. Forgive a father for wanting to reassure himself. I had hoped to relieve your mother of some anxiety. She alternates between bouts of worry and, what shall I call them, spurts of disgust? Her Catholic upbringing has instilled in her an oppressive absolutism unknown to a nominally Episcopalian Turley. I fear you have inherited some of her sense of mankind's unworthiness, especially men's, without even having had to set foot in Sacred Heart except for your Grandfather Riordan's funeral. Leaving her church to marry me may have only embedded her proprieties all the deeper. Your mother sees right through the hypocrisies of Lily Turley Lee and her flock of harpies, as she calls them, but she feels inferior despite that and dreads their gatherings so much she concocts a new white lie each time, so I attend alone. However, I can still enjoy myself. I hunt with several of the men, and we have plenty in common if we stay off politics. I do need a little society! And as you know from my letters, I try in my own way to keep in touch with my son though I have never been the most attentive of fathers. I will not bother your lawyer or your trust officer again. Forgive my poor attempt at playing spy.

Love, Dad

Dear Son,

We have found an excellent doctor of the Freudian school, an old lady trained in Vienna before the war. It requires your mother to take the North Western downtown and walk across the Loop or take a cab, in bad weather, to Michigan Avenue. Both are challenges for her, but she is managing. She goes Friday afternoons by herself, and I meet her after work and drive her home with me. Sometimes we'll have dinner at a quiet restaurant. As long as it's only the two of us, she's fine. I wish I thought your presence would help her, but until careful therapy frees her of her anxieties and, I may even say, the torments that still possess her, I do not care to risk it. She knows I write you these short letters now and then and is glad I do, but she never asks for news. And what could I report? All I've had from you are the infrequent postcards at the office, not unlike the little letters you would write us from summer camp. I have those still in my files. Let me quote one: "Dear Mom and Dad, Camp is fun. We went to Crawling Stone Lake. I don't mind baseball so much now. I'm good at archery. Don't worry. Love, Will." What were we to make of such a missive! The "don't worry" and "don't mind so much" put your mother through the wringer, but she would never have told you so. I could drive out now to your not-so-remote county and easily track you down, couldn't I? But see how I respect your privacy, just as we knew better than to show up at camp and carry you straight home. You were a stubborn little boy and still are.

Love, Dad

Dear Son,

So I have at last retired, and I'm not yet sixty! But it is a means to have more time up north. If I stay home with your mother, I earn the right to more trips to hunt and fish. That's our bargain. My compadres are all taking more time off. We're not so young anymore and plan to get in as much as we still can. Of course, their wives are delighted to get them out of the house. Not so your mother, but she makes no protest. The year with Dr. Olafsson has brought her a modicum of self-assurance. She will even accompany me on occasion to the John Lee household. Your philandering cousin John Junior appears to have been entrapped. His wedding to a particularly statuesque and slightly older gal is set for the fall. She is just the sort your mother can't abide—ready with pleasantries to smooth out every awkwardness, perfect in everything from tennis to sailing Lake Michigan in fierce weather. Heartiness has always intimidated your mother. When she's safe back home you should hear her go on about the intrepid Eleanor. I've come to find humor in her neurosis now that any real danger is past. If only I could break the taboo concerning her son—that is where Dr. O. could make no progress. To see John Junior in his glory, or tamed at last, has merely cemented her sense of shame and irredeemable loss. I sometimes think you are to her a martyred Catholic saint whose wounds she cannot bear to contemplate. Don't take this letter amiss.

Love, Dad

When she read those lines Nancy began to ask, "Did his dad know about—" and then, "Would he have said that if he—"

Lawrence was reading the next letter and he could only shake his head at this strange unloving world they were discovering. But they both read on through the decade of the Sixties, the words this strangely eloquent and embittered father had written to his only child.

. . . She takes to her bed much of the day. There's an oxygen tank in the room, if necessary. Years of those Chesterfields you so loathed! You used to complain how the smoke hurt your eyes, but she would smoke away in sheer defiance. I knew better than to criticize her. You accept things in a marriage if you're to coexist. I also accepted her fears. You never knew it, but I'll confess it now: there was a baby before you, but it was stillborn, a boy, a Tom Junior, as you're surely glad you never had to be. But after you, she would try no more. She had been terrified through that second pregnancy though your actual birth came comparatively easily. Unlike what your Aunt Lily went through with your Cousin John. I imagine my sister's increased grandeur is the result of never having been able to bear another child. So what have my own Momma and Poppa Turley to see from heaven? A son whose only son has hid himself away from prying eyes and is unlikely ever to perpetuate the family name and a daughter who bore only one nasty thing that's now married to a first-class bitch (says your mother). If Eleanor should bring forth young there may yet be some future for the gene pool! But don't count on it. She's nearing forty. Do you understand now why I spend as much time as possible in woods and streams? . . .

. . . I have enjoyed needling my brother-in-law with the R. C. in the White House. Of course, I backed Stevenson as long as possible, but for the sake of annoying big John I'll be sticking up for the Catholic from now on. "Appointed his own brother attorney general!" says my outraged sister, "it's the clannishness we all feared." "Some clan we are!" I shot back. Your poor mother slipped out of the room. See what fun you're missing, son? . . .

. . . Is it worth my writing to you any longer? Why do I do it? Your intermittent postcards scarcely warrant replies. They do not appear to be written in recrimination.

There's nothing for me even to dig into! They are as mild as mild can be. Why do you bother to write them? Some residual sense of duty to a parent you never intend to see again? No, they are not painful to me, and to your mother I can elaborate on them without being required to proffer evidence. She will not look at your written hand. "I couldn't bear it," she tells me. Does she allow herself to miss you? I believe she does not. Ah, this letter is turning into a catechism! I must ask myself the questions you and she will not answer for me. I live in a vacuum. She sits and reads, I mill about the house until such time as I may join my fellow men for a patch of the real life. Would you know anything of that? Don't answer! . . .

. . . We were quite lost in a terrific snowstorm. The ice was firm but cracking where the current rushed mad and furious beneath, so we snowshoed with care. It's a cruel climate, a forbidding landscape in winter. We were more watchful of each other because of it, though tempers grew short—a strange confluence of impatience and concern. Why should I write you of this? . . .

. . . You have a new little cousin, a third John Lee. May he break the curse of generations of Republicans! I don't mean to be flippant, but I've lately been rejoicing to watch the elder Lees writhe in psychic pain as Mr. Johnson rides roughshod over the last defenders of bigotry and impoverishment, triumphing like FDR redux. Do you care about politics out there in your monk's cell? Do you even know what's happening? Did you mark the assassination of Malcolm X, the Selma march, the Watts riots? Am I writing mere gibberish to you? I will ask no more questions, only to be answered with your I-am-fine's and your people-here-are-kind's and your don't-worry's. God dammit, it's nine whole years, eight since we've seen you. I know the damage that was done back then, and I know what your mother said when you returned from visiting that grave. Yes, I heard it from the other room. "And what did you do there, spit on it or kneel?" There, I've caused you to hear it again. But it's been my question as well. What did you do, son? I must send off this letter before I think better of it . . .

. . . Your mother's health has stabilized. Littlest John has been to visit, not with his tennis-playing sailboat-sailing mother, I may say, but with his nanny, who wheels him down Ridge Avenue in his buggy. Your mother actually waves from the window, and in they come. I have a suspicion she hopes to alienate his affections. A great aunt may subvert the pretensions of a grandmother. My dear Madgie is showing some invulnerability at last. She even had a kind word for the bitch mother. It has reached us that John Junior is up to his old tricks as he might well be, having been roped and branded by a lady four years his senior. She'll take to drink, no doubt. These athletic gals may have the capacity when they're young, but now what? Age, age, age! And you are thirty-one if a day. Never fear, we will predecease you, to use your country lawyer's term. Why not rewrite your legacy? Leave it all to John III! He's the only family blood worthy of respect (so far anyway), a smiling baby knowing only that he sees love in his great aunt's eyes and in the arms of his black-skinned nanny, and even perhaps from his tennis-and-golfing mom and his wildcatting dad. No, from his dad it's rather a challenge, an expectation that he must amount to something someday, but not too soon, kid, it's my turn still. Is that what you saw in my eyes, William Riordan Turley? Or did you see nothing at all? The shifting eyes of a forest beast or the vacant stare of a river fish? I'm poetizing in my old age. I've been informed that I am at the beginning stage of Parkinson's disease. There, I have said it . . .

. . . This war will be the downfall of my beloved president. I must turn against him, for he cannot bomb from one hand and feed from the other. I've become obsessed. I can hear your cousin John cheering, "War! It's the way it works! What's wrong with LBJ? Why not go all out? What's holding him back?" So what ground has an old Democrat like me to stand on? Ah, I forgot, you don't care about these things. Like your mother you will say, "I'm keeping up with my reading." You have become for me a specter haunting a past world. Your war should have been Korea. You were the right age and had put off college anyway. A medical deferment from your private humiliation, I soon learned. That was perhaps a better war. Who knows? Your late lamented benefactor survived it only to die in a stupid brawl off the base through no fault of his own. Ha! Some other drunken soldier gone berserk, the Korean hookers egging them on! I never had to go to war. Two years older and I might have. And I could have done more in the next one than kept the home fires burning. John Junior just squeaked in, even got overseas, and came back worse than before. You were only twelve. We do not see big John anymore. He's in his sickbed and wants visitors, but Lily and I only speak on the phone and in words of one syllable . . .

. . . I'm shakier of late. Your mother needs her oxygen quite constantly. Littlest John cheers her up with his babble. His nanny is practically your mother's only adult company. She was always more comfortable with black women. She knows the inequities they suffer and admires their strength. It is an earned strength, she says, not the coddled strength of the country club class we otherwise must associate with and to which we ourselves, I confess, belong. There are riots in Detroit. Did you know that? Am I the only person who tells you of the world outside? I hate what you have done to yourself over these thirteen unlucky years. Go from us, if you must, but put your pain toward some good use! I refuse to believe that what was done to you has crippled you forever. What you allowed to be done! That's what I can't—oh, I should have snatched you by the scruff of your neck and hauled you off to some hospital for cases like yours. I should have spent every penny it took. But Dr. Olafsson once told your mother there was nothing she or I could have said or done to keep you willingly at home because what we had already done and said could never be taken back. Her task was only to help your mother know her own self that she might now do and say freely what she alone truly wanted to say and do. The therapy, I admit, largely failed. After a bit more than a year my Madgie did not choose to continue. Perhaps she had only then begun to approach the heart of her problem. I was not allowed to inquire but confined my curiosity to what she might choose to tell me. That was the deal we struck when first she agreed to go. When she terminated, I was given no answers. If it is any comfort now, I will admit that your part in her illness was probably smaller than it may have seemed to you. You had not the sole power to undermine your mother's place in the world. I undoubtedly had a bit more power and her parents and brother Billy—damn him!—even more, and who knows who else? At least, when you kill a deer in the North Woods you know straight away what you have done . . .

. . . As you may detect, my handwriting is not what it once was. I will keep this brief. It has been a year of deaths, 1968, mark it. I myself may not outlast it. Or I may die with the decade. You are reaching the middle of your young life, son. By my reckoning, you are now precisely a third of a century old, and I have just reached two-thirds. Twice your age, too young to disappear. Perhaps your mother will be blessed with the biblical three score and ten, if blessed it would be. You would not recognize us, I so shaky, she so breathless. All too young, all too soon— will I be moved to write you ever again? When did your last card arrive, months ago? The office forwards my mail, a trickle including your occasional reports that I must hide from dear Madgie. Here is one stashed in my desk drawer: "Dear Dad, I have finally done as you suggested. Mr. Sturtevant has drafted a new document. I have no needs beyond shelter, sustenance, and my books. There will be plenty left over at some distant date for littlest John. Love, William." Is that the last I shall ever hear from my own child? A postcard for even the mailman to read while I continue to seal my letters . . .

. . .Winters are harder for us. Lily is at last a widow, a condition she has always aspired to. We talk on the phone from across the village. Her grandson is five now and tramps through the snow with his nanny and his little sister Abigail to bring cheer to Great Aunt Madgie and Great Uncle Tom. The former he loves for her squeals of delight, the latter he somewhat shies away from, as well he might. I made you shy away, didn't I, when you were little, but why then did we never fight? Why was it your mother you fought with? The two of you and your mutual stubbornness! You could be childishly cruel to her, insulting, belittling, and she could nag you and worry and recriminate, even long before the disaster. I wasn't home enough. All I am is home now, never to see my Tahquamenon! Do you remember your summer camp's canoe trip to Crawling Stone Lake? You were scared to be so far from home but had fun because you were supposed to. Didn't you once look up from paddling and see the world's beauty in its forests and lakes? That you have holed yourself up for over thirteen years! But I may yet see you again. I'm only sixty-seven. The far-flung Riordans are of little help with your mother. It all devolves on me, and what good am I? This stinking business . . .

It all came to an end with a last "Love, Dad." Lawrence and Nancy sat in silence. He stuffed the letters back into the manila envelope and set it on the coffee table then leaned back into Nancy's arms and reached his around her. After some time he said, "I think his father was only half in the wrong. I came to like him better."

"He suffered, too," said Nancy.

"And he sure had a way with words," Lawrence said, "though we don't really know what happened with Pitchley."

"But we know something now about Will's poor mom," said Nancy. "And his letter from summer camp nearly broke my heart."

At the Courthouse

I
t was one month to the day since Mr. Turley had slipped on the ice on his front walk and cracked open his skull and died. Word came to the bank that the will had been accepted by the court, and what had in fact been true from the moment of death was now duly registered at the courthouse. These days a county of dwindling population cannot employ its own exclusive judge but must share him or, quite often, her with a neighboring county or two, so Sinnissippi's criminal cases go up to Winnebago, its civil cases down to Lee, and the traveling probate court sits in Rockvale only intermittently. The Sinnissippi Courthouse is a three-story limestone-and-brick structure in the middle of the square, larger than it now needs to be and somewhat dilapidated but too much of a nineteenth century landmark to be supplanted by an efficient single-level facility. The uppermost floor is heated only by hot air rising from below and houses the county historical society's artifacts and records. Lawrence Huggins had begun again to contemplate finding some space up there large enough to receive the Turley collection.

When Rod Strite called with the legal news, there was other news of more import on everyone's mind. The Illinois State Senate had indeed convicted the governor of the charges against him and was removing him from office. "Not a good day for the name Rod," said the lawyer, "eh, Mr. Huggins? But justice marches on! It's Governor Quinn now, altogether a better man. What a state we live in! But anyways, well, it's worked out beautifully for you and the doctor. When you're ready to revise your own wills, here I am, if I may be so presumptuous."

"You've been very helpful, Rod," said Lawrence, "and you'll certainly hear more from us."

"Oh, by the way," Rod said, "the woman from Ryleston Properties will be calling, but I advise you not to sell yet. The market's bound to heat up."

"We have no intention of selling," Lawrence said.

"It's the sort of house I'd like to afford some day myself," said Rod Strite. "It's what I dream of—that, and a wife and kids."

"You'll get there," Lawrence assured him. He was fond of the young man, but of course they had their family lawyer in Chicago who took care of Cousin Trudy and it would be disloyal to switch.

"Oh, one more thing," said Rod. "The court clerk has Mr. Turley's last package the post office forwarded to us. Not that you need another book! We opened it to be sure it wasn't a treasure for the appraiser's list. It's just a tattered paperback called *Canary in a Cathouse*, but it didn't look salacious. It's by Kurt Vonnegut. His books are everywhere. Well, I hate to cut this short, but—"

After their warm good-byes, Lawrence was soon striding up the long courthouse steps to the grand entry on the second floor. When he swung open the wide door he heard the young clerk and three secretaries buzzing behind the front desk. It took a minute for them to notice him.

"You've heard the news from Springfield, Mr. Huggins?"

"Yes, I'm relieved it's over."

"It was like a reality show," said one of the older women.

"Better than," said the other, "because it actually's real. Those shows aren't really reality."

"We've got all your paperwork done, Mr. Huggins," said the clerk. "The judge passed it in before she left. Funny, that house used to belong to a judge. My dad knew old Mrs. Gale. Judge Gale was ours full-time. Now the courtroom mostly sits empty except for meetings."

"It's just not practical," said the younger woman. "It's like we all go to the Riparian mall. I don't suppose our IGA can last."

"We need a grocery store here," said the second of the older women. "Some of us folks wouldn't be able to get over there."

"You'll always have the bank," Lawrence declared. "Say, Mr. Logsdon, what's going on upstairs these days—the history rooms?" He had at last recalled the young man's name, though his given name eluded him.

"Want me to unlock?" the clerk suggested. Lawrence told him not to bother, but Logsdon foisted the key on him and said he could go look around at his leisure, few people ever did, and meanwhile he would make a copy of the documents so he would not have to send them by registered mail.

The wooden stairs creaked with each of Lawrence's footfalls. He and Nancy had gone up once, shortly after they arrived in town, but the display cases and framed pictures had meant little to them then. Now that they had made a home here they might touch him more closely. From below came a cheerful, "Switch on the lights at the top, sir."

The landing circled the building's rotunda, which rose to a squat dome that lit up sky blue when Lawrence flicked the switch. He went to the door directly opposite, which accepted the key, and opened it into the large room above the court chambers downstairs with smaller rooms off to left and right above the offices. Lawrence noticed first the flag from the Civil War years with its thirty-four stars and the manikin in the musty blue uniform of a Union soldier. He glanced into the glass-top cabinets displaying rifles and pistols and badges and medals and caps and knives. Another cabinet held open diaries and pages of requisitions and accounting sheets in faded ink hardly legible in the light from the dim bulbs suspended in ceramic tulips from the high ceiling.

Lawrence moved on to the farthest room to look for what he remembered were early maps and surveys and daguerreotypes of grim settlers' faces and the cabinet devoted to the station on the Underground Railroad in a farmhouse attic. This had moved Nancy when they first came upon it, especially the scrap of a diary resting on green felt that read, when Lawrence leaned in close and squinted: "Moses passed three days here before Zeke could take him upriver in the skiff by moonlight for fear of bountymen." Something in Lawrence shook, not his heart or stomach but something more like his kidneys, if that were possible.

He moved along to examine the wall chart showing the positions of the Federal and Sac troops before the battle at Stillman's Run. He suddenly wondered why he was here then remembered he had meant to search for an empty room.

There was none beyond this one, and the locked door led only to the hall, so he strolled back through the nineteenth century to the room at the opposite end of the little museum. It was a mishmash of artifacts from the homier decade of the 1890s, a school desk, a doll's house, a cradle, ladies' dresses on dressmaker's dummies, family portraits on canvas and in posed photographs behind glass. There were no black faces to be seen.

Beyond the other locked hall door was a small one leading to an empty closet, so that was the end of that. But it was dry and clear in this room with the late afternoon sun in the west windows. It would make a lovely reading room. The entire county museum could easily be accommodated in the other two rooms, and this one could be filled floor-to-ceiling with books. Lawrence paced off the walls and calculated the height that a library ladder could reach. Ten thousand volumes might indeed fit. The room was four times the size of any of Will's rooms and the ceilings nearly twice as high. Library tables could also hold some books. Only the handsome old hardbacks need be displayed at eye level. The paperbacks and newer books would go up top, even behind cupboard doors. They, Lawrence and Nancy Huggins, could endow the place, the William Turley Memorial Reading Room—a soft carpet, some deep leather chairs, Henry Settle to build the shelves—it would be no less often visited than the other history rooms and be waiting here for the unusual young soul, like Will, in search of a haven.

How long had he been standing there? Lawrence felt foolish and promptly tucked his dream away. Locking up and making his way back down the stairs, he could hear the older women chattering and the younger piping in with "I don't believe that" and "No, he couldn't have!" Mr. Logsdon came out across the rotunda to take the key and present Lawrence with the copy of all the documentation, now duly recorded, of his and Nancy's title to 17 Phelps Street, Rockvale Township, County of Sinnissippi, State of Illinois, to keep on file with the documentation of their earlier purchase of number 19, and he handed him also the old paperback, Will's last online purchase. The talk behind the front desk was still of the crimes and misdemeanors of former Governor Rod Blagojevich.

No sooner was Lawrence back at his own desk than the woman from Ryleston Properties was on the phone. She was simply calling to say she would send him the appraiser's report if he was interested. "Of course, it's conservatively valued for tax purposes, but it will give you some idea, Mr. Huggins. If you should consider selling in the spring, we could give our own opinion of value and set a higher asking price, but maybe you'll be renting it out or using it for an equity loan?"

"We have to think this through carefully," said Lawrence.

"The antiques, you'll see from the appraisal, are actually worth something, as I figured they would be. The octagon table, for instance—a thousand dollars! Naturally, you may wish to keep such a fine piece. It can only increase in value. As for the books, they estimated there were some eight thousand and put them down at two thousand dollars, but I doubt you could realize twenty-five cents a book for most of them. Those nicer old sets, on the other hand, are in some demand from designers. Lydia Ryleston, Mr. Ryleston's wife, does interiors over here, and I know she'd be eager to come take a look if you don't find a dealer for the lot. People love that look of old sets of books in a study. And Lydia would go wild for the judge's glass-fronted bookcases."

"We'll keep her in mind," Lawrence said gently, "but Nancy and I have yet to make up our minds about anything. If we do decide to sell, we'll be sure to . . ." He made all the polite promises and apologies and evasions and even took down Lydia Ryleston's email and thanked Serena for all she had done, knowing she had been well paid for it from the estate.

"It must be nice to start afresh," she said in closing, "the taxes and fees all taken care of. It's usually the tightest moment for new homeowners, but you've only got to step right in." Her laugh, perhaps, carried a note of resentment that Lawrence quickly covered with a laugh of his own, followed by one last promise to stay in touch.

But they will never be required to deal with this Serena again, or her boss's wife Lydia, or anyone at Stark, Weber, Brennheim, and Braun unless they so chose. Even jolly young Rod Strite could evaporate from their lives now.

THEIR IMPERSONATIONS

opied documents and flimsy paperback in hand, Lawrence walked briskly home to find Nancy napping on the sofa. He tried to tiptoe past, but she caught him, yawned, and said, "No appointments, so I came home and lay down to make up for last night. I didn't sleep too well. I got to thinking about Will and his parents, and that got me missing Chloe and I started worrying over her and what this Deet is really like, and my mind kept on running."

Lawrence caused her to scrunch over against the back cushions so he could squeeze in by her side and take her hand.

"Sometimes in the night, Lawrence, I wake up feeling so alone out here. Not alone, because I'm with you, but the two of us alone in such a strange place for us to be. Then it sets me remembering old Will and how for years and years and years he was alone out here too. It goes round and round in my mind."

"He had his books."

"But he left his parents and never saw them again. I'm sure they hadn't treated him right, and I know that his cousin John did terrible things and then something especially shameful happened. But I can't forgive Will for never going home."

"He went that one time to visit his friend's grave."

"But never again. I'm guessing it all had to do with his friend dying. We thought it was in the Korean War, but his dad said it was just some bar brawl. I don't know what it was about that Caleb Pitchley, but don't you suppose he really loved Will, not necessarily in a sexual way, I mean, but Will must've been his very best friend in the world—"

"To be his beneficiary," said Lawrence.

"Because they weren't relations. Maybe he'd protected Will from the cousin."

"I still can't spot Will as being homosexual," Lawrence said.

"We wouldn't say so now, but back then maybe it wouldn't have been the way we're thinking of it. They may not have even known it about themselves, just boys with romantic longings—"

"There've been gay people all along, Nancy."

"I know that, but I mean Will and this Caleb might've been all confused. And their parents got suspicious and accused one or the other? I wanted to tell you this, but I thought you'd—"

"Not understand? No, I understand."

"Because why else would a young soldier take out an insurance policy like that? Didn't he have family? It's not as if he was expecting to die, well, maybe in the war and it was a gallant gesture to make for his friend."

"If Pitchley was killed in combat it might not have paid out. Can you even insure a combat soldier? I suppose for a high enough premium."

"But he didn't die in combat."

"I could Google the name and maybe find out more," Lawrence said.

Nancy leaned up on her elbow so she could look straight at his face instead of seeing him at an angle above her. She touched her hand to his cheek. "I don't want to know more about Caleb Pitchley," she said, "or more about William Turley either. Lawrence, I want us to go back home again. I want it left purely that something good happened years ago between two young men and the one who lived has now passed it on to us because we'd been good to him. Can't we sell the house and go back home?"

"We have jobs, honey. These are shaky times."

"Couldn't you ask someone in Chicago? Ask Hub or Hirsch or one of those guys in the know. The bank's always moving people about."

"I don't want to risk it now. Better times are coming."

"But I could go right back. They need me, they've said so. In the city we'd see more of Chloe. She'd come down. Oh, Lawrence, let's call her, I need to hear her voice."

His arms went around her, and she hugged him back. "We'll be fine, honey. Okay, we'll call. But look what I've brought—Will's last book order and the copy of the deed from the courthouse. I was planning on celebrating by taking you out to the Basswood, and here you're already talking about selling."

"We could go out anyway," Nancy said with a wistful smile. "I suppose it's something to celebrate, owning two homes." Lawrence got the phone from its cradle in the front hall and brought it back so she could dial. After a moment she said, "It's the machine," but she was smiling at the sound of Chloe's voice. Then: "Hi, sweetie, your dads and I are going out to dinner, but we'll call tomorrow. Oh, we miss you so much! Couldn't you come down to visit some weekend? The house next door is officially ours now. You might have some ideas what to do with all the books. You could bring Deet. We love you, work hard."

"We love you," Lawrence said loud enough to be recorded too.

At the Basswood they were lucky enough to get the last empty booth by the fireplace where its imitation coals glowed and gas jets flamed. They each ordered a glass of house red and two pork loin specials from their familiar chubby waitress whose name was Annie. She turned out to be an in-law of the Stover clan, so there was talk of Millie and Elsie and Judy, and they all felt cheerful. "Mr. Bass will bring your wines, and I'll get you started on salads," she said.

Somehow Will Turley's past rose once again in Nancy's thoughts and she had to say how she still wished she understood old Will.

"I thought you wanted to leave him behind," Lawrence said. "Look, it's wisest not to speculate on his sexual orientation."

"I wasn't thinking of that. I know it makes you uncomfortable."

"It doesn't make me uncomfortable. But it's pointless now."

"What I wish though," Nancy said, "is that I could remember more things he said over supper. I wish I'd written them down at the time."

"They're gone," Lawrence said.

"So," Nancy said suddenly, "here we are at this table. You be the Hugginses on that side, and I'll be Will Turley on this. It's how I role-play with kids sometimes. I pretend to be them, and they get to play doctor. They come out with questions they wouldn't ask otherwise."

"It's embarrassing, Nancy."

"Try?"

But after salad and some wine and while he was buttering a roll, Lawrence looked up and said, "So tell me, Will—wait, am I being the doctor or the patient?"

"You're being us. Go on, I might remember something."

With a conniving grin Lawrence said, "So, Will, what's it been like living in this town all these years? You must've seen some big changes."

"I don't see much if I can help it, Dr. Huggins," said Nancy.

"Call me Nancy," joked Lawrence.

"It sounds disrespectful, but Nancy it is!—See, Lawrence, I remember him saying something about being respectful.—So, Nancy," she resumed in character, "I take great care not to see too much. The town doesn't change except for the generations proliferating—isn't that a Will word?—and then they move away. There's fewer people here now than when I arrived. There was the old County Bank, Mr. Huggins."

"Lawrence," said Lawrence. "Say, Will, have you been up to the history rooms in the courthouse? Nancy and I took a look once."

"I avoid the courthouse," Nancy said. "I don't much like the law."

"But you live in the judge's house."

"I don't like the law because it's no good to most people."

"—Did he ever say that, Nancy?—"

She nodded but stayed in her role. "I had dealings with the law once. Didn't do much good for me."

"Is that the case?" Lawrence found himself imagining Nancy would somehow come out with the truth of what happened to Will, but she said only what he would have said.

"Oh, you wouldn't want to know. It's tedious and past fixing. I was talking about the broader principle, that people presume to pass judgment on each other."

"—Yes," Lawrence said, "I remember he said that. Nancy, how did you do it?"

"It came to me. I probably won't be able to think of anything more.—"

But Lawrence went on: "Will, we pass judgment all the time. It's how we have a civilization. It's taken some centuries, but we're getting better at it."

"You really think so? I prefer the people in books. And what do you think, Nancy?"

Lawrence had to answer. "But books also judge people, Will, and people have written the books."

"No, Nancy, I don't think of it like that. The people in books are like my children. You know what I mean, you're a mother."

"—I can't believe you're saying all this, honey."

"See, it's coming back. I remember when he talked about Chloe. 'You love your daughter,' he said. He could see it in our eyes when we said her name. 'She isn't a little girl now,' he said. Remember? 'You don't judge Chloe, you love her,' he said.—"

"We do have an opinion, though, on every little thing she does," said Lawrence to both dead Will and his living wife.

"An opinion is different, my dear neighbor—remember how he'd call us his dear neighbors?—and an opinion carries no penalty. It doesn't have the law behind it."

"—So what he was saying, honey, was that he could read his books and know they weren't factual about real people, they were made up, they were people beyond the reach of the Law."

"But in books you want the good people to win out."

"He didn't seem to care much about good and bad, Nancy. There was nothing he could do about the people in his sorts of books because they didn't really exist, so he could sit and read and watch and think without taking sides. Remember when he said he didn't glean information from books? *Glean* was one of his words. He said he lived in other people's lives. I thought he meant real historical people."

"But it's immoral not to care about the difference between right and wrong."

"We've always said he was no Christian," said Lawrence.

Annie brought their platters and warned they were hot then collected the salad bowls and asked if they wanted more rolls. Nancy said, "Oh, no thanks," and Annie looked a little crestfallen that their chit-chat had not revived, so she snuck away. "You're saying Will read his books in a moral vacuum, Lawrence?"

"I think he read them as if he was his own version of a god," Lawrence said. "He was the god of that house, and he filled it with all those people. He made them talk out loud. He could be anyone he met on the page, good or bad, right or wrong. I have a feeling he loved them all the way our Lord loves us."

"He was the strange lonely old man next door, Lawrence, who probably should've been in a psych ward, and whether it was from childhood trauma or a breakdown after his friend's death, these days we'd medicate him. And probably do his emotional life a disservice."

"I don't think he was crazy, honey. Remember how he spoke about race? It wasn't what you'd expect from a kindly old white man. It wasn't *color-is-only-skin-deep* or *I-don't-judge-you-by-the-color-of-your-skin.* He said race is a *characteristic.* That was the word. Race is an important characteristic," Lawrence said being William Turley again. "Race is one of those ways we know each other. It's a significant detail."

"How're we doing, folks?" said Annie coming to refill their water glasses.

"It's delicious, Annie," said Nancy.

"Pork loin's nice and juicy," Lawrence said, "and I'm a pushover for your garlic mashed potatoes."

"We'll be coming back when our daughter comes to visit," Nancy told her. "We're hoping she'll bring her new boyfriend."

That allowed Annie to revive their chat and stand by the table with her pitcher and ask about Chloe and pass on advice from what she was going through with her two teenage girls.

On their slow drive home Lawrence said, "Let's not do that again."

"The Basswood?"

"No, pretend to be Will. It was too odd."

"But I wish we remembered him better," said Nancy.

"Honey, first you want to leave him behind and I want to remember, then I want to leave him and you want to remember. Why aren't we ever on the same page about this?" He turned down the alley and jockeyed the Civic into the garage beside her Forester.

"He's gotten under our skin," Nancy said. "It's being out here so long without family. If Chloe doesn't come visit, we'll go to Chicago some weekend. I need to see old friends. I need some black faces. I can't wait until spring."

Before bed, Chloe returned their call. Nancy told her not to worry about them, but they did miss her every day and would even drive up as far as Madison and meet halfway for a Saturday lunch if she were not too swamped. Then Chloe said, "Actually how about the Presidents Day long weekend? I have four relatively free days, and so does Deet. His winter show will be over and all the tryouts for spring. You could finally meet him! And if you think it'd be weird, him staying with me in the house, you've got your other house he could sleep in. He'd like that. I mean he wouldn't like not sleeping with me—sorry, Moms—but he'd be less nervous about meeting you both."

"Deet's nervous?"

"Sure he's nervous! You should hear how I talk you two up. And he had to hear it all over again from Cousin Trudy."

Under the Cushion

ow Nancy and Lawrence had something to look forward to and in only two weeks. They always found that they got through their days particularly happily when they knew a reward was coming. It was how they had managed their move to Rockvale, knowing it was a step to a higher position for Lawrence back in the city. That was before the economy crumbled. But then came election season with much to hang their hopes on, and when it came out right, they had plenty more to look forward to, despite the prognostications of certain colleagues like Hirsch and Hub. Back in 2006, Hirsch had known when and where to move his personal investments. He had warned Lawrence in time, though the Huggins portfolio was hardly in his league, especially after putting Chloe through Northwestern and helping Trudy pay off her mortgage. Besides, Lawrence had always invested conservatively. He had lost very little and only had to keep working and take no long shot risks for them to have a secure retirement. And now, assuming they could find a buyer, William Turley's bequest would put them in fine shape.

It was a quiet weekend. Felipe Reyes knocked on the door Saturday morning to ask, with no new snow, if there was anything else he could do for them. Lawrence invited him to step inside.

"Who's that?" Nancy called from the kitchen.

"Honey, Felipe's asking if there's anything we need done."

She appeared wiping her hands on a kitchen towel and was properly introduced. Felipe removed his knit hat and shook hands with each of them. Nancy had never said more than a quiet hello before when he was taking care of the yard next door in the summer. "There'll definitely be something when we ever decide what to do over there," she said pointing out the window. "Do you do painting, Felipe?"

"Painting?"

"Interiors? Where there's wall space without any shelves, it could use a fresh coat."

"I do painting. He kept ladders in his shed."

"We should think about that, Lawrence."

"But anything here right now, honey? I tell you, Felipe, why don't I give you a twenty today for the next snowfall, and by the time it snows again my wife and I will have figured out what we could ask you to do."

"Thank you, mister."

"Do you have enough work in Rockvale? You work for lots of people?"

"Yes, lots of people. I have work."

"You have family here?" Nancy asked.

"I have family," Felipe said. "Not here, in Dubuque—father, mother, sister, brother, me, then little sister."

"They came up from Puerto Rico," said Lawrence though Nancy knew that.

"Villalba in the mountains," Felipe told them.

"However did you end up way out here?" Nancy asked.

Felipe scratched his hair to think a second then said, "Church. Not Catholic, my church, Church of God in Christ. You?"

"We go to the Methodist Church," Lawrence said.

Felipe tilted his light brown face and scratched at his hair but said nothing more.

"And where do you live?" Nancy asked.

"Mrs. Dickerson."

"He rents a room from her." Lawrence happened to know because Mrs. Dickerson had recently taken out an equity loan and mentioned her tenant. He was about to suggest that Felipe come in for coffee, but the Church of God in Christ had put him off, and after the little man left, Lawrence admitted it to Nancy.

"I know," she said, "but it would've been polite."

"I was afraid he might start proselytizing us. It's better to keep it on a professional basis."

With the Bears out of it and, for Chloe's sake, the Packers as well, Lawrence did not put much stake in Sunday's Super Bowl between Pittsburgh and Arizona, but he would go to the Van Inwegens' party and root with them for the Steelers. Lawrence had never been an obsessive sports fan, though he was attached to his Chicago teams and did like being part of a big civic event, thrilling or disappointing as seasons might go, but Nancy had no interest at all and begged off the party. It was always easy to make excuses for a doctor.

Lawrence noticed they had not been socializing much after all the Christmas parties, including their own for the bank's employees. January was when everyone retreated into cold and snow and back-to-school or vacations south for the lucky retired ones who could afford it. Now it was February. It would be awhile before the town came out of hibernation and they would be seeing the Pratts again and perhaps have Rose and Alexander Carron over for an evening. Right now it was too much work to get yourself moving. But barring a terrible storm, Chloe would soon be there, and she would help them decide what to do about the other house. She might say they should move over and sell their own, a home already in move-in condition. Besides, they could then have fun fixing up Will's house—Felipe painting, Henry Settle doing the carpentry. They could house more of the books in the judge's study if they shored up the floor with lally columns in the cellar and built stacks like a real library and then turned the front parlor into an elegant living room. They did not need two parlors. Upstairs, the front bedroom could be Chloe's, the middle their own, with Will's for guests and his reading room a study. As he drove across town and out to the Van Inwegens' old farmhouse up the bluff, Lawrence found himself imagining an entirely new manner of living for him and Nancy. He had been putting the pieces together so many different ways he was sure to find the right arrangement.

As the afternoon progressed at home, Nancy felt a similar restlessness, but she had no Super Bowl to take her mind off their uncertainties. She also looked to Chloe's presence as the decisive factor. They could plan nothing until she had walked through 17 Phelps Street with them. Nancy almost wished Deet was not coming, but then he might prove useful. Chloe would be on her best behavior and expect them to be on theirs for Deet. They would all four take everything seriously, no family squabbles, no tears. Unless Deet was some kind of oddball, though Gertrude Huggins had not found him so.

Nancy was sitting on the sofa wrapped in the afghan Lawrence's dear old cousin had knitted and trying to read a book called *Beka Lamb* by Zee Edgell. It was one of the Caribbean novels Chloe had given her for Christmas hoping to interest her mother in the writers she was working on. It was a nice enough book but without the kinds of characters Nancy could quite relate to. "It's not about relating to, Moms," Chloe had told her, "it's about getting outside yourself and seeing what else is out there in the world." But Nancy preferred a page-turning story with people she could imagine herself being or at least wanting to be, where she could care firsthand about what was happening to them. Chloe had reminded her that some of her own people came up from the Caribbean. Nancy knew it but felt the same way Lawrence did about that African writer he had tried to read. It was too foreign and the plot never quite went anywhere, at least not where you might expect. "I'm a doctor, sweetie," she had told her daughter. "I like to diagnose and heal. I don't like not to know what's going on, especially at the end. Your father, too," she said, "he's a money man, he wants things to add up on the plus side. We've got our limitations, sweetie, we're not scholarly like you." But Chloe said she made scholarly sound like a mental condition. Then they laughed and admitted they admired each other even if none of them quite knew what it was the others did with finances or medicine or literature.

Nancy lay her book down on the cushion beside her and decided to walk over next door and go through the house to see it fresh with Chloe's eyes. She stood right up, put on her coat and boots, and was out the door before stopping to wonder why she was doing this.

She had never herself slipped the key into the lock on the front door. She had never been in Will's house alone. Two days ago it had officially become theirs, but somehow they had not felt like going over to stake their claim. Were they afraid of seeing it differently? Yes, Nancy decided, she was a little afraid. But in the low-angled light it looked especially lovely to her. Chloe would find it lovely too—the intricately moulded woodwork, the polished floorboards, the smooth plaster ceilings painted bright by the setting sun, the brass ceiling fixtures aglow. The glass fronts on the judge's cabinets shone out like golden tablets. Nancy had barely set foot between the pocket doors when she was struck by the need to go upstairs to Will's reading room and try out his chairs, where neither of them had dared to sit down the other times they had inspected the property. I want to sit where he sat, Nancy told herself, I want to pretend to be Will looking out his window at the other house, ours, where those Hugginses live, to see what he would have seen.

At the top of the stairs she turned into the small room lined with the newer paperbacks where he had spent most of his waking hours, the room from which his voice could be heard on warm days behind the whir of the fan that stood silent now on the floor below the sill. Nancy raised the shade as far as it would go and looked across at her house with the shadow of Will's house creeping slowly up the brightly lit western side. Then she turned to light the standing lamp and sat herself down in the soft armchair but reached over to the rocker to pick up the last book he had been reading, left open where he stopped. She started to read aloud what came next, despite the chilly air in the old house. She had not thought to turn up the thermostat.

"'There is to me an odd pathos in the literature of vegetarianism. I remember the day when I read those periodicals and pamphlets with all the zest of hunger and poverty, vigorously seeking to persuade myself that flesh was an altogether superfluous, and even repulsive, food.'" Nancy mumbled, "What the hell is this?" But she lifted her voice again and read on. "'If ever such things fall under my eyes nowadays, I am touched with a half humorous compassion for the people whose necessity, not their will consents to this chemical view of diet. There comes before me a vision of certain vegetarian restaurants, where at a minin—' Minim?" Nancy said aloud. "'Where at a minim outlay, I have often enough made believe to satisfy my craving stomach; where I have swallowed "savoury cutlet," "vegetable steak," and I know not what windy insufficiencies tricked up under their specious names—'"

She could not read on. Zee Elledge or Edgell, or whoever that author was, sure made more sense than this. Nancy looked to the next chapter. It began: "Talking of vegetables, can the inhabited globe offer anything to vie with the English potato justly steamed?" Here were those potatoes again! What the hell was Will reading this for? It's not a cookbook. Is it supposed to be a story? *The Private Papers of Henry*

Ryecroft by George Gissing. So it's Henry Ryecroft's private papers, but George Gissing's the author, so it has to be fictional, but this is the most insane kind of story I ever read! Nancy snapped shut the old volume, almost angry at old Will himself for presenting her with such an absurdity. Well, maybe he had read all the more normal books, she thought. Maybe it was a blessing Will had died when he did. He was running out of his kinds of books, and living authors weren't dying fast enough to keep him supplied. Nancy had to laugh. She leaned back in the armchair and noticed how cold her fingers had grown and how much darker it was getting outside. The shadows of Will's house had reached far up their second floor. And now that she would be reading no more, she felt how annoyingly lumpy the chair cushion was. How had Will sat here for so many hours reading that crazy book? She stood and lifted up the cushion and pinched and poked at it, but it was soft enough. Then she saw, lying flat on the exposed cloth beneath, an envelope, business-size, white but yellowed with time and stuffed with folded papers—the lump she had been sitting on.

She almost did not dare pick it up, but then she had to. She replaced the cushion and sat back in the lamplight. Her fingers were trembling from cold and timorousness. She wished Lawrence was there but was glad he was not. She must first discover if this second envelope was something he should know about or if it would best be kept secret or maybe even destroyed. She was taking on a heavy responsibility. They had promised not to keep secrets from each other.

The papers inside were folded various ways, in fours or threes or sixes, stuffed in randomly, not neatly stacked like those in the manila envelope under the mattress. She did not know where to start, so she chose the one that stuck out farthest, unfolded it, and sat there reading.

"Slave: These are your orders. Clean every inch of my room top to bottom. Treat my combat boots with neatsfoot oil. Press my shirts, no ironing marks. And if I find one piece of grit in the sheets or a speck of grime on a windowsill or any dust under the bed or anywhere else you will be punished. I have laid traps to test you. If I find you have not discovered them and set things right, then the whip will really come down next time. This is how I train you. And you must be out of the house before my parents return. If they find you here without me, you will have hell to pay. Am I your hell? You decide. Destroy this note."

Nancy was trembling now—fingers, arms, shoulders, her heartbeat, and right down to her knees, her ankles. Aloud she said, "The cousin!" It scared her now to hear her voice in the empty house. She could see her breath hovering in the cold air. What kind of family had Will escaped from? How had he survived them? But now she was her doctor self again. She had studied childhood trauma. She had seen its effects in numb-faced little patients with shifting glances and fidgety hands, children who would not answer when asked a question, whose little lips could not form smiles. Even out here in Rockvale she had seen them and called in Janice Kimball, the county's pediatric social worker. The note she was holding was written in an older boy's sloppy hand, not a young one's carefully practiced alphabet. This was teenage boy writing but without the spelling mistakes or funny punctuation of a mere thug. How much older was John Jr. than Will? Nancy remembered there was a considerable age difference. Poor little Will!

She had to investigate further. I am his doctor, she told herself. She picked out a note folded over once and once again like a greeting card. Inside the first fold she found the same handwriting: "Turley! You are getting fat and lazy. You are the heaviest in our class. Kids laugh at you because of your big flabby body. Big boys—" Wait—*Our class?* Nancy wondered. Will and John were not in the same class. "—Big boys are supposed to be tough. You stink in football. They plow right over you. You're a cream puff! You lost us the game against Lake Forest. If I was coach I would not even let you on the field. Your pants fell down trying to make a tackle! You were hardly trying anyway. Anyone can outrun you. Everybody laughed. What they don't know is that you are my slave and later I got back at you for losing—"

Nancy had to open out the second fold to finish the sentence: "—us the game . . ." but her glance fell to the bottom of the page and a scrawled signature she could not at first decipher. Then she realized it said "Pitchley." These were letters from his best friend. She picked out another to see if the handwriting was the same. Each piece she unfolded, whether in pen or pencil, was in the schoolboy scrawl of Caleb Pitchley. He signed one: "Caleb, your only friend in the world. Do not have another friend. I own you." And some began "My slave" or "To my slave" and even "To the slave."

How had this ever begun? Two boys playing a game? And she had imagined they loved each other! This Caleb Pitchley was a young monster. Nancy could not read much more of what he had written. She unfolded papers, glanced over them, caught phrases—"You don't deserve . . ." "You're going to get it bad . . ." "It's almost time for your punishment . . ."—and folded them up again. She wanted to crumple the papers or tear them in pieces, but for now she stuffed each one back in the envelope. She was glad of her years of training, her years serving a rough neighborhood, the hard things she had learned.

Every day, reading in this chair, Will had sat on this lump of letters from his tormenter as he had slept every night on those letters from his father, his past always with him. The letters lay there as he read and slept. Why had he preserved them? And why—Nancy had to ask herself now because, in the shock of reading that nasty scrawl, she had forgotten—why had Caleb Pitchley endowed the man he called his slave with an inheritance? Surely he had expected to come home from Korea, to marry, to make his own children his beneficiaries, to live a long prosperous life, and his victim would never know what a flash of good conscience might once have brought him.

As chilled as her fingers were, Nancy looked again for the paper where she had read the words "You're going to get it—" and had to unfold a few before she found it: "You're going to get it bad. It's what you deserve for being so weak. Ten lashes! You don't ever do anything. You sit reading your stupid books when you should be serving me. Get it?" Nancy unfolded one more: "You are lucky that I own you. What would you be without me? What would you ever have? Nothing. Never forget it."

Nancy had read case histories of terrible abuse between adolescent boys, of teenage gangs, of street fights, and in history books of lynchings in small country towns. She had heard Granny Jo tell tales of Barbuda learned from her own grandmother, who had come from there. Nancy had seen that movie when she was a girl. Had it set her on a path toward medicine? "I want to be a doctor," she had told her mother when she was no more than twelve. Or was it only her irresponsible brother Marvin she had wanted to outdo? Why was she sitting here now in the cold, with this old yellow envelope on her lap, thinking about these things? She was no scared little girl, though she could recall her youthful fear of what cruel people had done and her own anger at people who did nothing to stop them. Why had Will not defended himself? Maybe, after all this, he still loved that awful Caleb. Poor Will was heavy and soft and no good at sports and quiet and bookish, and here came this strong young thug who declared he owned him. Nancy pictured Caleb in motorcycle boots and black leather jacket like those greasy white juvenile delinquents in old movies on TV in her high school days. Or maybe Caleb was just a scared skinny kid like anyone else, but playing a terrible game. Will was probably embarrassed to be fat and never took off his shirt in front of anyone. But would no doctor have ever seen the scars? Will must have finally been found out. His parents must have intervened. Or the Pitchleys, or the police. Then Caleb had volunteered for the Army. That was how bad kids often got off. Nancy had figured it out. And Caleb was a rich white boy with all the advantages. That is, until the night in Korea when he was too drunk to save himself.

She would explain it all to Lawrence when he came home from the Super Bowl party. She turned off the reading lamp, stood up, and tucked the envelope in the big pocket of her coat, but on her way down the dark stairs she concluded that she would never tell Lawrence. She stopped halfway on the landing and felt suddenly surrounded, above and below, by William Turley's books. He had left this house to his neighbors. If he had gotten sick and known he was dying, he would have had time to destroy the evidence hidden under mattress and cushion, but instead Nancy had uncovered his secrets. Now she knew that the house was truly theirs alone. Will had left them his books, not to be sold or donated or dispersed, but to belong only to Lawrence and Nancy Huggins, because they were descended from people once enslaved, and they would know, as if in their blood, how all those thousands of stories had been a haven for him, even if they never would read a single volume. Every one of those books, even the one he had not finished that criticized vegetarian cookery of all things, Nancy decided, every one of those books surrounding her now, all those stories of the past, stories from the dead, those imaginings, not themselves true but dreamed up by true people, mostly white people, she acknowledged, and more foreigners than Americans, but every word on every page had comforted William Turley by making him part of other people's lives, even their sadnesses, the cruelties they endured—he was not alone with his pain, in his mourning. More books could still arrive. Chloe did not have to wait for a writer to die. Chloe would add to the collection for them, and Deet would wander through the rooms and exclaim in amazement, "Your parents must be something to own all these books!" And that was why Will had wanted his neighbors to be his heirs.

Nancy came carefully down the dark stairs and, by the streetlight shining faintly through the amber glass on either side of it, found the front door. She made sure it locked behind her. She touched the envelope in her pocket. It would go into her briefcase and straight to her office at the hospital. She loved Lawrence so much, but she could not let him see what she had found. He was happier leaving Will's past unexamined. Let him think kindly of Caleb Pitchley. Nancy was stronger than her husband, she was a doctor, and Lawrence need not know that Will's benefactor was also the inflicter of his suffering. Lawrence thought that love and hate were opposing forces. He did not wish to see how entangled they were. He was the better Christian, Nancy thought, but she had come privately to another conclusion.

So when Lawrence came home cheered by Pittsburgh's victory over Arizona, cheered mostly because the Van Inwegens were cheered and their party had ended in high spirits, Nancy told him how lovely the other house had looked with the declining sunlight shining through the tall windows and how she had seen it all afresh with Chloe's eyes and decided they should leave it exactly as it was, whether they moved over or rented it out. The books simply came with the house. Other houses had wallpaper and pictures on the walls, but that one had books. A renter would just have to live with them, and they themselves would live with them, if they chose to move over and rent out this one.

To her surprise, cheerful Lawrence said, "I'm beginning to think so, too. Besides, it will be simpler and certainly cheaper to leave them where they are."

WHICH HOUSE?

But they still had no idea where they should live. They agreed to wait for Chloe's visit and, in the meantime, tried not to trouble their minds. Nancy had Caleb Pitchley's letters stowed away deep in the cabinet, where she kept the plastic cars and plush animals as rewards for brave children, and wondered if she would ever tell Lawrence about them, but he seemed resolved to speculate no further about Will Turley's scars. There was always a question of how much to tell anyone, even your spouse, about anything. Nancy was cautious with patients and their parents. Keeping spirits up was part of any cure. She never deceived anyone but stayed calm and confident to allay worries and fears. She believed that any affliction could be managed, except for death itself. Having attended dying children in her city practice, she recognized mere life for the blessing it was. She and Lawrence were well, their Chloe was well. Will Turley had transcended his teenage trauma well into his seventies in a strange but not a tragic life. They were lucky to have known him, not for his bequest but for his example. Nancy resolved she should not have panicked or felt so alone and desperate to return to their Chicago. Day by day, she would take heart in what they had. As for Lawrence, a bank stabilization was in the works, the president's people were on top of it now, there would be another stimulus, the economy would slowly improve—but they must be patient. "We're definitely not putting either house on this market," Lawrence had told her, "whatever Chloe S. Huggins may recommend, and we don't even have to be in a rush to rent one of them out. We're among the lucky ones, honey."

One bright noon hour he strolled home to make himself lunch and was intercepted by Joe Etnyre coming down the walk from 21 Phelps, where the polite but distant O'Flahertys lived. Joe handed him the mail. "But hey, get this, Mr. Huggins, Eddie Boyce said for me to start delivering to 17 again, you know, circulars and stuff, because Turley's box is discontinued, and actually here's a letter addressed to you at the other house, see, 'The Huggins Family.' It's from VT, that's Vermont. I never delivered one from Vermont before. You been out there?"

"It's from Mr. Turley's cousin, the one who inherited his money."

"So it wasn't you? That was the talk around town."

"Heavens no, my wife and I hardly knew Mr. Turley."

"But you got his house."

"The cousin off in Vermont didn't want it," Lawrence said hoping to sidetrack any local resentment, "so we made a deal."

"So which house are you going to live in? You can't live in both. I'd take the judge's if I was you. It's got more class. I was looking forward to going up to the door for the first time ever, but I guess you've got your letter now."

"Here," said Lawrence handing back the letter, "you can make the first delivery." He followed Joe up Will's walk, up the steps, onto the porch, and then realized there was, of course, no mailbox or slot in the door.

Joe puffed out his cheeks in disappointment. "Hey, what's this whippoorwill for?" he asked.

"We don't really know."

"From the street I always figured it was a nameplate saying 'Turley' like my dad has 'Etnyre' on his."

"Did no one ever come up these steps?"

"Let me tell you, Mr. Huggins, that old man was the privatest old man ever. Nobody wanted to disturb him."

"Were they afraid of him?"

Joe swung his mailbag around to the other shoulder. "This thing gets heavier despite I'm emptying it out. Explain me that! No, but some people you can tell just don't want to be disturbed."

Lawrence took out his key ring. "Want a peek inside?"

"You mean I could?"

Lawrence opened the door, and the postman stepped inside and said, "Holy Christ! Look at all them books!"

"That's only one room. They're in every room but the kitchen."

"Holy Christ!" Joe said again. "I better not track slush in here." But he peered into the judge's study and said, "This is awesome. This is what the guy did all day in here? Like the wise old man of Rockvale, huh? Can I tell people?"

"Mrs. Gitchell's seen it, so I'm sure word is out."

"Christ, these are more books practically than the library. You better start reading, Mr. Huggins!" He handed over some circulars and the letter, and they parted out again on the sidewalk.

Back at home, Lawrence made himself a ham and cheese sandwich and a cup of tea, set the bills for 19 Phelps aside, and opened the envelope from Vermont. He found two single-spaced typed pages like that long letter to Rod Strite.

Feb 2, 2009
Dear Huggins Family,

Excuse me for intruding on your privacy, and I promise not to expect you to strike up a correspondence with a total stranger, but we are linked through the death of my relative, Mr. William Turley, formerly of this address, whom I never knew and whom, I presume, you knew well. My condolences. I was glad to learn through Mr. Strite, his lawyer, that you have inherited the house where my first cousin (once removed) lived all those years in seclusion. I regret that my parents, or perhaps I should limit it to my father, had been so estranged from Cousin William and never spoke of him. Neither did my great uncle and aunt, his own parents, who were otherwise very sweet to me when I was little. I used to toddle up the street to visit them and loved my Great Aunt Madgie especially. It's so long ago since that generation died off, and my own poor mother died only three years ago and my little sister Abby dealt with all the family effects because my wife Sue and I live up here in the boonies like hermits. Maybe some of Cousin William seeped into my blood. Anyway the point is, my sister was going through old family letters and came upon one from Great Uncle Tom to his sister, my grandmother, and it's the only thing Abby ever learned about Cousin William, so she sent it to me because of the inheritance, and I've typed you out a copy (no Xerox up here) thinking it may be of interest. Not that it really explains anything, but hold onto your hat. Sue found it upsetting. Now with everyone dead, the real truth of things is lost for good, unless William told you more. If so, perhaps you could let me know. It's not that I need answers, but family history was always an interest of mine despite having staked out a life for us and our kids up here in the mountains. I even found out that some Turleys settled originally near Lake Champlain before the Revolution. Anyway Cousin William has given us more to be grateful for than my own father the big capitalist ever did. Redistribution of wealth to the counterculture bums, says my little sister who doesn't need more than she's already got. I didn't intend to go on like this, but Sue says when I get on the old Smith Corona I can't stop myself. Good thing we don't get Internet up here. One last thing: I wish all the Huggins family health and happiness in your new house, whoever you may be, and if there's some small item of Cousin William's you might send as a keepsake to remind us of him, a photo, a book, his hat or something, nothing of value, just a token, we would love to have it. Sue says to promise I won't bother you again. But have my sincere thanks for being my unknown old cousin's friendly neighbors.

John Lee III

Lawrence had consumed his sandwich, brushed some fallen crumbs back onto the plate, taken a last sip of tea, and now turned to the second page.

June 26, 1955
Dear Lily,

I hope you're all enjoying the clear waters of Wipigaki. I would dearly love to be swimming up there right now, but Madgie is in no condition to travel. The departure of the son we thought we could count on has come as a terrific blow. I am more philosophical. That the unmentionable one's accidental death should have given Will his independence from us is one of the great ironies. We have done all we could to understand and help our son, but as you know from having dealt with John Junior, young males can be willful creatures, thoughtless of parents and all the proprieties and even of their own futures. Your John was never kind to Will. I don't blame you for it, but you must admit, Lily, he tyrannized over his little cousin unmercifully. Eight years difference in age should have protected our boy, but not by John's lights. He once made Will lie flat while he stood astride his head then jumped up as if to bring his boots down on Will's face but then split his legs apart just in time. He once commanded Will to run down a hillside while he fired his pistol right over his head. Who knows what other acts set in motion that sense of unworthiness in Will that led to the shame we uncovered too late for any remedy. Had our boy turned to us earlier and pledged never again to allow such things as would later occur, Madgie could have come through better, would have been stronger. Why would Will not confide in us? Are we so judgmental? Whatever he suffered, our son was too proud—Will is stubborn, defiant when it comes to us, can even seem unloving. I may say he deeply hurt his mother long before this last unexpected twist that has overridden any financial suasion we may have tried. I have only now brought myself to write him as kindly a letter as I could muster. I trust our estrangement will not last forever. All we have now is a post box number in a small town out in the country. Oh, to be in the North Woods where it's cool and breezy and I could deposit Madgie at Wipigaki and go on up to my sparkling Tahquamenon and forget our present sadness! I trust the elder John is well and young John is wildcatting less. He is turning thirty, isn't he? For better or worse, we all were long married by then.

Love, Tom

P.S. John Lee III here again! I hesitate to interpret this letter, and Sue is opposed to me even sending it because for all we know you may be evangelical homophobes, but my take is that Uncle Tom is saying that my dad made Cousin William feel so bad about himself as a little boy that it turned him queer, because that's what even enlightened people used to think was how it happened, and that Aunt Madgie was so nervous about what people would think because her William got way too queer for their taste, given the social norms of the day, and then his boyfriend, namely this Pitchley, got killed in the Korean War and left him all that money, and William was so broken up he went to live like a celibate monk for the remainder of his days, to punish the whole family. Doesn't that sound plausible? No, Sue, I'm sending this, they'll deal with it. (That's what I just told her.)

Lawrence sat and stared at the typing. Some letters were fainter than others, some were doubled where John Lee had hit the wrong key and typed over them, a few letters dropped below or hopped above the line. Lawrence had not received a letter like this since his college days at Roosevelt. He did not want to involve himself in a correspondence with this third John Lee, who seemed to have few boundaries. He supposed if you came from privilege and went off to live in the mountains, you might end up a bit loony.

Lawrence was glad he had come home for lunch and read the letter first so he could prepare Nancy for it. Or perhaps he need not show it to her at all. If only John Lee had asked for a memento of his deceased cousin and left it at that, but his speculations did make some sense, as far as they went. What this younger John could not know was that his father, John Junior, had in fact done much worse than pretending to stomp on Will's face when he was little or shoot a pistol over his head. Lawrence and Nancy knew the whole truth, but Nancy should not have to learn these minor new details. She hated to hear of children being hurt, children hurting each other. Rather she should be thinking now only of how Will's best friend Caleb had eventually rescued him from his older cousin and given him the means, though tragically through an early death, for Will to escape his tormenting family. Better for Nancy to think of the kind friend, or lover—it did not make Lawrence uncomfortable to call him that, whatever Nancy said, but she didn't need to read John Lee's notions on the subject either— yes, to think only of the friend who had redeemed Will's tortured childhood like a good doctor. And all those books Will had read, books surely sometimes about death, they must have served well to help him in his long years of faithful mourning.

So Lawrence put the two pages back in the envelope and took it with him back to the bank where he housed it for now in his bottom desk drawer, and when he and Nancy met again at home he said as casually as he could, "Oh, honey, I got a call from old Rod, who heard from the Vermont cousins. They wondered if we might send some small item, a book or a picture, he said, something of Will's as a keepsake. I have their address. What should we choose?"

"They're not second-guessing us having the house?"

"No, honey, they just want a memento, something small. They never knew him."

"Not a book," Nancy said. "We're keeping them all, and we have no pictures of Will. They'll never know what he looked like."

"A hat?"

"He was wearing his only hat, Lawrence."

"But isn't there one book, honey? The last one he was reading, the potato book."

"Especially not that one! That one's so peculiar, but I'm going to finish it for him. I am! I'm going to make it my own personal memorial service that he never got."

"What about the one by his bed still in plastic? He never got around to it."

"Maybe," Nancy said. She took her husband's hand and walked him into the kitchen to get supper going. "Technically then, it isn't part of the William Turley Collection," she said. "I wonder why he put it off for so long."

"We'll send it," said Lawrence. "I'll enclose a note saying it's the book Will intended to read next that we found on his bedside table. The saleslip has his name on it. They'll like that. And it's nicer than that tattered old paperback sent after he died."

"You came home for lunch!" Nancy said when she found the crumb-covered plate in the sink. "I wish I had your executive schedule. I had a frantic day."

"Then after we eat," Lawrence said, "let's go next door and sit with all our books for a while and get used to having them. We can both squeeze into that big armchair in the front parlor. We could even turn off the lights and christen the place, if you know what I mean."

"Lawrence Huggins!"

"It may help us decide where to live."

"You do want to move over there, don't you! You want to live in the judge's house."

He shrugged teasingly but with no idea yet which house might best shelter their love for each other until the time came when they could at last go home to Chicago.

Their Daughter

The next week, after the stabilization had been announced, Lawrence found a long-stemmed red rose on his desk with a Post-it reading "Phew!" He suspected Helen Van Inwegen, but she had received one, too, and pointed at Millie Stover.

"Millie, you shouldn't spend your money on us like that."

"Oh, I'll be getting my own dozen, Mr. Huggins, on Saturday from you know who."

"Poor Henry," said Helen.

"I'd prefer he got me chocolates."

Lawrence made no sign of having forgotten Valentine's Day but wrote himself a note to call Cox's to deliver a small bouquet to Helen and something special to Nancy, and he would pick up chocolates for the tellers from Mr. Doyle on his lunch hour. And Chloe! If she and Deet had an announcement to make it would be the perfect day for it. He called the Basswood to reserve a riverside table for Saturday night.

On Friday, Lawrence and Nancy were both home an hour early to prepare supper and warm up Will's house for Deet. Nancy was more nervous than Lawrence, who was eager to see his Chloe no matter what man she dragged along. But Nancy feared their daughter was at a point that would determine her whole future. It was at Chloe's age that Nancy had found Lawrence.

A lime green VW, the real version of the Bugs Nancy gave out to little boys, pulled up at 19 Phelps Street. A tall very dark-skinned man in a Russian fur hat and glasses stepped out and lifted the hatch to grab their bags, and there was Chloe in her dark blue parka taking her bag from him so they could hold hands coming up the walk. Lawrence and Nancy had to kiss her and squeeze her tight even before shutting the door on the cold and letting her introduce them to the handsome young man, who doffed his hat revealing, as foretold, a smooth-shaven head. He removed his glasses to wipe the fog off with his handkerchief before shaking hands. "Now I see you!" he said.

With spiked hot cider in mugs in the living room, it all went smoothly. Nancy could see that Lawrence liked Deet because Deet clearly adored Chloe, and Nancy liked Deet for that but also because he already seemed to like the two of them. She was not nervous now at all. There was plenty to hear about the long drive down and how Deet's GPS had a British accent and about the pile of freshman papers Chloe had finished marking before they left. She was free for three whole days and did not plan on even cracking a book.

They quizzed Deet about his theatrical activities. He would not come up for tenure for several more years, but they had given him the spring show, *The Birds* by Aristophanes, which he would stage in spectacular African robes and headgear with drumming and chanting for the choruses. "You guys have to come up," Chloe said, "you have to!" Lawrence promised, though the play sounded far-fetched when Deet explained what it was about.

"You would've liked the show they just finished," Chloe said, "Chekhov's *Three Sisters*, about being stuck out in the country and wishing you lived in Moscow."

"We hardly wish we lived in Moscow," said Lawrence.

Chloe made a long-suffering eye-roll. "Chicago, Dads? Duh."

Nancy asked where Deet got his odd name. He said it was short for Dietrich because his parents had him when his father was stationed in Germany, but he had to spell it with two Es or it would look like "diet" in English.

"Like Marlene Dietrich," said Lawrence.

"Actually, it's for a classical baritone my mom likes. She's a music teacher. It's how I got into theater, by singing in high school shows. Then I went to Oberlin and studied directing. I'm not much of a performer really."

Lawrence was relieved. He had doubts about an actor as his daughter's possible mate. Nancy excused herself to the kitchen, and

Lawrence told stories of Chloe growing up and bragged about her achievements at Northwestern, and then over supper they heard first-hand reports of Cousin Trudy and the rest of them back home and about Deet's family in Akron, Ohio. All consideration of the house next door had to wait until it came time to show Deet his sleeping quarters.

"He doesn't mind, Moms," Chloe said while they were putting on their coats in the hall. Deet snatched up his suitcase, and out they went.

"It's just there's only that one twin bed in the guest room," Nancy reiterated.

"It's fine, Moms, hush."

Lawrence, ahead with Deet, said, "Prepare yourself for a lot of books. You may be up all night looking them over. There are plays as well."

"Chloe warned me about the books."

When they turned on the lights for the tour, Deet was clearly overwhelmed. "I had no idea, Mr. Huggins."

"This is craziness," Chloe said. "I had to see it to believe it! But what a cool old house. Look at the floors. And the chandeliers! You definitely have to move over here."

"Uh-oh," said her mother.

Deet was running a finger along the titles on the German shelves. "You have quite the extensive collection here, Mr. Huggins."

"It's alphabetized by author," Lawrence said, "and arranged by country. Downstairs here are all the older books and upstairs the more modern ones."

"You mean there's more?"

"The old man sure was anal," said Chloe.

"Let's show you your room first," Nancy said on the stairs, so they trooped up and into Will's bedroom, where she had remade the bed with their own linens. The unread book by the bed was already with the Lees. They had immediately received a thank you card of a snowy scene with wolves that read: "Dear Huggins Family: I don't know if we'll get around to reading it, but it sure means a lot to me and Sue. If you're ever in the East come say hello. John Lee III." Nancy asked if Deet would be comfortable enough.

"This is great, Mrs. Huggins, I mean Doctor—"

"Nancy and Lawrence from here on."

"I just call them Moms and Dads to keep it simple," Chloe said.

"And here's the old-fashioned bathroom, but with fresh towels," Nancy continued. "I brought over some of ours. Mr. Turley's were ancient. He was quite tidy, but he never bought anything new."

"There's something Chekhovian about him," Deet said. "This house is a character study."

"I predicted he'd love it, Dads."

"We'll leave you two here to explore," said Lawrence. "Come along, Dr. Huggins."

On their way down the stairs Nancy called back, "Feel free to leave the lights on. I don't want you scared in a big dark house."

Back in their own well-lit one, they sat on the sofa to discuss the merits of Dietrich Hartsfield and declared him a welcome prospective son-in-law.

"I just hope Chloe's mature enough for him," Nancy said.

"She's more mature when we're not around," said Lawrence.

Chloe came back soon enough and flopped between them. "He's wiped and so am I. We decided we'd save it for Valentine's Day tomorrow."

"Chloe!"

"So, Moms, you passed, and Dads passed, and I'm assuming Deet passed. But the more I think about that crazy house over there—" Chloe shook her head. "I mean, it's a beautiful place underneath all the books, and in Chicago it'd be worth a million-plus with those moldings and inlaid floors. Out here though, I don't know. Deet would move right in if it was in Appleton, books and all. It'd make a great setting for a wedding reception. Shut up! We have no plans, I'm just talking. He doesn't get the whole William Turley story yet, and I must say it's pretty weird, but Deet likes how Russian it all is."

"Why do you both keep talking about Russians?" asked her father.

"Russians in books and plays, I mean. They tend to be eccentric. I'm not talking about Communists, I'm talking about the nineteenth century. Deet was impressed you had the whole set of Chekhov stories in thirteen volumes. He counted. He's into Chekhov right now because of *Three Sisters*. The drama department gets to actually do things, and in the English department we only talk about them. I told him you said Mr. Turley had read every book over there aloud. Deet thinks it must've been like a one-man theater with a one-man audience. That's what's so Russian about it—you know, *Notes from Underground* and how it influenced Ralph Ellison. Remember I gave you *Invisible Man?* There's a lot of the Russians in African-American literature. Their serfs might as well have been slaves. It was a pre-industrial world."

"Chloe, you certainly are rattling on," said Nancy.

"Oh dear," said their daughter taking a long breath. "See, Moms and Dads, he's someone I can truly share things with. I never had a boyfriend like him. They were all into sports and economics—sorry, Dads, no offense."

"Your Jake wanted to be a doctor," Nancy reminded her.

"Not a chance! Total party boy. But, you see, I'm actually into all this stuff. I want to teach it to the coming generation. Deet wants to direct plays that connect. Wait till you see what he's doing with *The Birds*. It's going to be amazing. He's very cerebral, but he's got so much life in him. He studies human character. I bet he's over there psyching out Mr. Turley right now. He was showing me one Russian novel you have over there about a man who never gets out of bed or something like that. It could almost be about Mr. Turley. And he's so excited about my work on Achebe. Have you read *Things Fall Apart* yet? It's about when a new civilization clashes with an old one. I'll send you some others about modern Nigeria that might be easier. I mean, fuck the big screen TV, Dads! That *Timon of Athens* production we saw in Chicago, you couldn't achieve that effect on TV. When it's in front of your eyes, or even only inside your head when you're reading it, it's so alive! So Deet's psyching Mr. Turley out. He's going to understand him, I can tell. But I mean, I'm so grateful to you two for putting me through college and putting up with my stupid boyfriends in the past and all that teenage shit I used to pull. So now I want to share the fruits of your labors with you."

"You are the fruit of our labors, sweetie," Lawrence said with one arm wrapping around her to match Nancy's from the other side.

"See, Achebe has this essay about the novelist as teacher. It's at the heart of my work. I'll send it to you. It's how in Nigeria the novelist still has the role of teacher. We're so fucking decadent over here, we want our quick buzz and off we go. He doesn't mean teacher as in preacher or professor, he means teacher as artist, showing things you can't learn any other way. Like how a culture creates itself through subtle complex edgy truths, the sorts only artists can tell. It's never a simple lesson, it's a whole organic thing. It can be the ancient Greeks, like Aristophanes. Theater in Africa has more of the role of ancient Greek theater for a community as a whole, for the culture. Like, take this satire on dreaming of some perfect state you can never reach, like heaven, the birds' cloudland, even if it's not real. It's the if-only-we-were-in-Moscow sort of thing. No, but instead you have to look at what is. That's both plays' point. You were thinking, by his reading, Mr. Turley escaped from what is, but Deet thinks he was diving deep into it, all those lives in all those books, not escaping things but facing them."

"I've never heard our daughter go on like this," Nancy said. "She isn't on something, is she?"

"Look at my eyes, doc. Are the pupils dilated? Come on, can't I tell my own folks what's going on in my head?"

"I was kidding, honey."

Chloe took a slower breath and said, "But now I'm truly wiped, too. We're all going to bed."

*****

Valentine's Day was a success—the flowers that arrived, the chocolate assortment Chloe and Deet had brought with them, the stroll around town with a quick lunch at the Greek's and, after a drive in the Forester to show Deet the rest of Sinnissippi County, the unsophisticated cuisine at the Basswood followed by Chloe's private visit over at the other house. She crept in late while her parents pretended to be asleep.

Sunday morning, they all went to church and heard Pastor Miller preach dully about the various kinds of love, ending, of course, with "God Is Love," which is how the Norwegian playwright Ibsen also ended one of his plays, Deet informed them. Then the two lovebirds drove off to stay with friends in Madison to break up their trip north.

On Monday, Lawrence had a quiet Presidents Day alone at home trying to plow through *Things Fall Apart*, but Nancy had to be at work.

Their Neighbor

It took another week for them to come to some short-term decisions. When Henry Settle stopped by the bank to see Millie, Lawrence called him into his office and asked if he could come give an estimate on some small improvements to the judge's house and maybe get Gerry Waite to come check out the wiring.

The following Saturday, Felipe was out there shoveling both walks and sets of steps and the paths around back and out to Will's shed and their own garage. Then Henry showed up, and Lawrence and Nancy took him over to inspect, for the first time, his own father's handiwork, the blond oak bookshelves in the front parlor and the reddish cherrywood ones in the dining room, also the simple pine shelves upstairs. "All so beautifully rabbeted and dadoed," he said. "No one builds like this anymore, Mr. Huggins. Good old Pa!" Nancy went down to Will's kitchen to brew a pot of tea. "It'd cost a fortune now, the custom cabinetry. You'd best not mess with them. They're the real thing. Of course, I could fit some drawers or stick on pine doors up here if you want to use them for cupboards, but then what would you do with all them books?"

"We've tried everything to find them a proper home," Lawrence said, "but it looks like they're ours for good."

Nancy called them down and yelled out back to invite Felipe inside, and the four of them sat at Will's dining table while Nancy poured out tea from his old teapot. Felipe did not have much to say but kept glancing at the wall of Russian novels.

"Anyways, books make the shelves look useful," Henry said. "Shelves need something on them. Books even provide insulation, those on the outside walls at least. And these inner ones are bearing walls and won't sag the floors. I sure got to hand it to Pa. Now that he can't work no more, he's the reader in the family. I ain't got his patience."

"Patience," Felipe said into his teacup.

"But I like seeing books around me," Henry said. "I go to the library on Saturdays for the magazines. I was there this morning."

"We asked at the library and the school and the church and even over at the college," Nancy said. "An interior decorator wanted some, but we didn't think Will would appreciate that."

"Will Turley haunts me," said Henry. "I still feel what it was to lug him up into my truck." Felipe's pointy face was going almost pale. "I'll never forget it," Henry said. "I was the last person to see him still breathing. I feel I somehow knew him."

"Grace of God," said Felipe.

Gerry Waite knocked on the kitchen door. When Lawrence let him in, he predicted that the wiring had not been updated since the Fifties. "Have a cup of tea first, Gerry," said Nancy. "I'm heading back to the other house to catch up on my email."

"Which is the other house now?" Lawrence asked.

"The one we're not in at the moment," said Nancy. "You fellows will be all right?"

"I'll get Felipe to make us an estimate on giving the walls where there's no shelves a nice fresh coat of white paint," Lawrence said, "and I'll see what these other gentlemen think needs to be done to the place."

*****

After Nancy had been up in her home office awhile checking lab results and going over the latest medical reports, Lawrence also came back home and planted himself on the sofa in the bay window where Susie Gitchell used to see Mrs. Henshaw, the bank manager's widow, sitting and sewing. He actually had no work to do, nothing pressing anyway, but he needed to think. He had suggested to Felipe, when they walked down the well-sanded walk, that he might think about putting in a garden over there in the spring. Felipe said Mr. Turley never asked him to garden, just mow and clip, but he liked growing flowers. Lawrence knew that the old man who had lived there so many years had once done the gardening himself. Young Susie Gitchell, or whatever her maiden name had been, would watch him from across the street through the branches of the maple tree that was now a stump and dream up romantic stories. She was to become the town's librarian. Meanwhile, on the South Side of Chicago, a boy was born named Lawrence Huggins, and a few years later in the Andersonville neighborhood a girl was born named Nancy Sublette. By a fortunate coincidence, they happened to meet at a party in the year 1981 and later married, while she was still in medical school. They had worked hard in the city and were blessed in 1984 with a daughter they called Chloe, a name they had heard and liked without knowing where it came from or why it was spelled so strangely. Lawrence had done quite well for them all, through his hard work and intelligence and because it was a time when the bank, the Marquette Bank before it became AmTrust, was at last ready for a young black man, just as Nancy's first hospital was ready for a black woman doctor. This would not have happened so easily a generation earlier. Neither would it have happened that their daughter would now be taking her Ph.D. in literature—well, all of it might have happened, but it would have been considerably more difficult, and Lawrence did not know if he or Nancy, or even Chloe, would have had the strength of character to put up the necessary fight. He thought of Gertrude Huggins and what more she might have accomplished if she had been born into a later time. She was a brave woman. Lawrence and Nancy were the beneficiaries of the bravery of their forebears. Their forebears had to be brave. They would not have survived without being brave. That was their legacy to Lawrence and Nancy. Poor William Turley had little of that bravery. He had been beaten down by a bullying cousin and retreated into his books, and even if Dietrich Hartsfield said that reading was some deeper way of living, Lawrence knew it was so only if you took from it what you could and went out into life itself and did something. It was a fine thing to have read all those books of his, but Will should have been like Chloe and Deet and taught his knowledge to others. Or if he was so shy, he could have read his books to the blind! All that reading aloud with no tape recorder—think of the service he could have rendered! His voice had vanished into the air, unheard by all but himself. William Turley was not born unworthy, as his cousin John had caused him to feel, but he had proved himself unworthy by not reading his books into a tape recorder for the blind, if reading was all he could do with his life. Caleb Pitchley had certainly never insured his own life so that his friend would disappear into a country town and be as good as dead to his family, even to the people of Rockvale where he lived, year upon year. Deet might talk about underground, invisible men—that paperback of Chloe's was there on the shelf by the TV, Lawrence hadn't read it yet—but Deet was certainly not invisible, he did not spend his life in bed like some sleepy Russian. Deet put on plays for live audiences. Nancy and Lawrence would be going up to Appleton in April to see the ancient Greek one, but mostly to see their Chloe. She had made reservations at the Comfort Suites, and they would get to meet all her friends. Dammit, Will Turley could have gone off to college somewhere! Why didn't he? Lawrence had had enough of Will Turley, who had squandered his advantages and then imposed himself on their lives forever with his house and his books that they could not unload and that Nancy had, despite all reason, become attached to in some mysterious way—to the idea of them more than to the actual books on those beautifully carpentered shelves. Ownership, that was what they had now, ownership of an unwieldy library his wife was determined to preserve intact. Yet it was indeed a lovely old house, and as long as they had to live in Rockvale and prices kept falling, they had best hold onto it. It was costing them practically nothing. Maybe they could offer it at a low rent to Henry Settle, who now lived in a small apartment above Cox's Flower Shop. His disabled pa could come sit in the front parlor and read whatever he liked. The back bedroom, bath, and kitchen were enough for a single fellow, and he could study his father's carpentry in the remaining rooms and learn something. I see how my mind works, Lawrence admitted to himself. He had sat here working up resentment at poor old Will and now was figuring out how to take in some modest rent money. But worse, he had kept a secret from Nancy. He hoped he was right not to have shown her Tom Turley's letter to his sister or John Lee's to the Hugginses, though it meant breaking their solemn promise always to tell each other everything.

Upstairs, Nancy was at the computer staring at the new screensaver Chloe had sent of her own desk, piled high with books by Tutuola and Ekwensi. Nancy had finished catching up on email, and now, like Lawrence, she simply needed to think. She stood and went to the window, knelt on the carpet, and lay her cheek against the sill to wonder about what was to come. We have done well, she thought, but will Chloe? She and Deet may be safe for now at the university, but that's not the world, and here we are with two houses in a safe quiet white folks' town with no immediate chances of going home to Chicago, and the economy may never go back up. All the good may have come too late. *But lucky, lucky, lucky,* she said to herself, watching the shadows cast on the snow by the other house as the winter sun drew west. *Lawrence does not know what I know,* she thought. He does not know what degree of cruelty an only friend is capable of reaching, what brutalities the young may allow themselves to enact. Some kinds of wounds may never close, though we all go on and are glad to be alive. What a strange form of cure those books provided our old neighbor! If only medicine could be as effective. Then she remembered sitting across from Will at supper, serving him a plate of meatloaf and mashed potatoes and collard greens and cornbread, remembered him ladling out the steaming gravy, spreading butter on his bread, and smiling up at her and Lawrence, and she could hear his voice say, "Thank you for this feast. There's nothing nicer than your good meals, Nancy, and nothing finer than your fine red wine, Lawrence. You are such kind people. I wish I could repay you." What Nancy thought she had replied was: "Don't be silly, Will, it's our pleasure having you home with us."

quale [kwa-lay]; *Eng.* n 1. A property (such as hardness) considered apart from things that have that property. 2. A property that is experienced as distinct from any source it may have in a physical object. *Ital.* pron.a. 1. Which, what. 2. Who. 3. Some. 4. As, just as.

www.ingramcontent.com/pod-product-compliance
Lightning Source LLC
Chambersburg PA
CBHW031113260626
47172CB00001B/340